FROM MEN TO MONSTERS

FROM
MEN
TO
MONSTERS
A WALES AND LOUISVILLE SAGA
T. STYLES

Are You On Our Email List?

Sign up on our website

www.thecartelpublications.com

CHECK OUT OTHER TITLES BY THE CARTEL PUBLICATIONS

SHYT LIST 1: BE CAREFUL WHO YOU CROSS
SHYT LIST 2: LOOSE CANNON
SHYT LIST 3: AND A CHILD SHALL LEAVE THEM
SHYT LIST 4: CHILDREN OF THE WRONGED
SHYT LIST 5: SMOKIN' CRAZIES THE FINALE'
PITBULLS IN A SKIRT 1
PITBULLS IN A SKIRT 2
PITBULLS IN A SKIRT 3: THE RISE OF LIL C
PITBULLS IN A SKIRT 4: KILLER KLAN
PITBULLS IN A SKIRT 5: THE FALL FROM GRACE
POISON 1
POISON 2
VICTORIA'S SECRET
HELL RAZOR HONEYS 1
HELL RAZOR HONEYS 2
BLACK AND UGLY
BLACK AND UGLY AS EVER
MISS WAYNE & THE QUEENS OF DC (LGBTQ+)
BLACK AND THE UGLIEST
A HUSTLER'S SON
A HUSTLER'S SON 2
THE FACE THAT LAUNCHED A THOUSAND BULLETS
YEAR OF THE CRACKMOM
THE UNUSUAL SUSPECTS
LA FAMILIA DIVIDED
RAUNCHY
RAUNCHY 2: MAD'S LOVE
RAUNCHY 3: JAYDEN'S PASSION
MAD MAXXX: CHILDREN OF THE CATACOMBS (EXTRA RAUNCHY)
KALI: RAUNCHY RELIVED: THE MILLER FAMILY
REVERSED
QUITA'S DAYSCARE CENTER
QUITA'S DAYSCARE CENTER 2
DEAD HEADS
DRUNK & HOT GIRLS
PRETTY KINGS
PRETTY KINGS 2: SCARLETT'S FEVER
PRETTY KINGS 3: DENIM'S BLUES
PRETTY KINGS 4: RACE'S RAGE
HERSBAND MATERIAL (LGBTQ+)
UPSCALE KITTENS
WAKE & BAKE BOYS
YOUNG & DUMB
YOUNG & DUMB: VYCE'S GETBACK
TRANNY 911 (LGBTQ+)
TRANNY 911: DIXIE'S RISE (LGBTQ+)
FIRST COMES LOVE, THEN COMES MURDER
LUXURY TAX
THE LYING KING
CRAZY KIND OF LOVE
SILENCE OF THE NINE

Silence of The Nine II: Let There Be Blood
Silence of The Nine III
Prison Throne
Goon
Hoetic Justice
And They Call Me God
The Ungrateful Bastards
Lipstick Dom (LGBTQ+)
A School of Dolls (LGBTQ+)
Skeezers
Skeezers 2
You Kissed Me Now I Own You
Nefarious
Redbone 3: The Rise Of The Fold
The Fold
Clown Niggas
The One You Shouldn't Trust
Cold As Ice
The Whore The Wind Blew My Way
She Brings The Worst Kind
The House That Crack Built
The House That Crack Built 2: Russo & Amina
The House That Crack Built 3: Reggie & Tamika
The House That Crack Built 4: Reggie & Amina
Level Up (LGBTQ+)
Villains: It's Savage Season
Gay For My Bae (LGBTQ+)
WAR
WAR 2
WAR 3
WAR 4
WAR 5
WAR 6
WAR 7
Madjesty vs. Jayden: Short Story
You Left Me No Choice
Truce: A War Saga (War 8)
Truce 2: The War Of The Lou's (War 9)
An Ace And Walid Very, Very Bad Christmas (War 10)
Truce 3: Sins of The Fathers (War 11)
Truce 4: The Finale (War 12)
Ask The Streets For Mercy
Treason
Treason 2
Hersband Material 2 (LGBTQ+)
The Gods Of Everything Else (War 13)
The Gods Of Everything Else 2 (War 14)
Treason 3
An Ugly Girl's Diary
The Gods Of Everything Else 3 (War 15)
An Ugly Girl's Diary 2
King Dom (LGBTQ+)
The Gods Of Everything Else 4 (War 16)
Raunchy: The Monsters Who Raised Harmony
An Ugly Girl's Diary 3

FROM MEN TO MONSTERS (WAR 17)
THE END. HOW TO WRITE A BESTSELLING NOVEL IN 30 DAYS

WWW.THECARTELPUBLICATIONS.COM

FROM MEN TO MONSTERS

By

T. STYLES

PUBLISHER'S NOTE:
This book is a work of fiction. Names, characters, businesses,
Organizations, places, events and incidents are the product of the
Author's imagination or are used fictionally. Any resemblance of
Actual persons, living or dead, events, or locales are entirely coincidental.

Library of Congress Control Number: 2024905581

ISBN 10: 1948373939

ISBN 13: 978-1948373937

Cover Design: Book Slut Girl

First Edition

Printed in the United States of America

BOOKS IN ORDER

1. WAR
2. WAR 2
3. WAR 3
4. WAR 4
5. WAR 5
6. WAR 6
7. WAR 7
8. TRUCE
9. TRUCE 2
10. AN ACE & WALID VERY, VERY BAD CHRISTMAS
11. TRUCE 3
12. TRUCE 4
13. THE GODS OF EVERYTHING ELSE
14. THE GODS OF EVERYTHING ELSE 2
15. THE GODS OF EVERYTHING ELSE 3
16. THE GODS OF EVERYTHING ELSE 4
17. FROM MEN TO MONSTERS

What up Fam,

During this first quarter of 2024, I hope you guys are doing aight! For anyone going through something at the moment, I pray that God hears and answers your prayers. 🙏

FROM MEN TO MONSTERS...Babbbbyyyyyyyyy.... When I tell y'all this book had me in a chokehold...that's exactly what I mean! Now, I know I'm biased and ANYTIME I get to catch up with my favorite families, (Wales' & Lou's) I'm too excited. That being said, this latest contribution to the WAR series will probably go down as one of the 'best of' in T. Styles' bibliography, hands down. Once this story gets to unraveling, you will be gagged! Strap in!

Now, let's shift our focus and keep in line with tradition. In this novel, we want to give love to,

RuPaul Charles

RuPaul Andre Charles is an **ICON**! A LEGENDARY Drag Queen, TV Personality, Host, Singer, Dancer,

Actor, Producer & Writer. He does a little bit of it all! RuPaul's competition series, ***"RuPaul's Drag Race"*** has been nominated and received countless Emmy's. The show is not only empowering but has changed so many lives. RuPaul has recently dropped a new book entitled, *The House of Hidden Meanings: A Memoir* and as a huge fan, I can't wait to dive into it.

Ok, I've kept you from this masterful work long enough! Get to it and I'll catch you in the next one!

Peace & Blessings!

C. Wash
Vice President
The Cartel Publications
www.thecartelpublications.com
www.facebook.com/authortstyles
www.facebook.com/Publishercwash
Instagram: Publishercwash
Instagram: Authortstyles
www.twitter.com/cartelbooks
www.facebook.com/cartelpublications
www.theelitewritersacademy.com
Follow us on IG: Cartelpublications

Follow our Movies on IG: Cartelurbancinema

#CartelPublications

#UrbanFiction

#PrayForCece

#RuPaulCharles

#FROMMENTOMONSTERS

PROLOGUE

"Can I refuse the offer?"

Nestled in an embrace of voluptuous green trees, a dark structure seemed out of place. A black box like house stood strong, its silhouette bold against the money green forest. The body crafted from slats of dark wood, seemed to drink up the light.

Sexy.

Alluring.

Yet scary.

Directly in front of this one hundred-million-dollar estate, a helipad lay. With just enough space for two.

Suddenly the trees begin to rumble, releasing their leaves like feathers in the wind. The silence was now shattered by the approach of two huge mechanical beasts. Closer they came, silver, gleaming in the sunlight. Their blades slicing through the air like machetes.

Once both landed, the engines were cut, and the roar faded. Revealing four powerful men in black expensive suits, their skin, a palette of vanilla and almond. Once they descended from the vessels, they moved with the confidence of those who always, *always*, got what they wanted.

In their world money wasn't just power, it was law.

And those who disobeyed them would find out how far they would go to keep things under their command.

As the bosses approached the house, the black box revealed its jaws and electric door swung open, as armed guards ushered them through their property.

MOMENTS EARLIER

Sharon Drexel sat in front of a large window which expanded from the floor to the ceiling, right to left. From her viewpoint, she couldn't see anything but trees. Sweat covered her brown skin, and the recent Dominican blowout she received was starting to reverse to the natural off black 4C pattern of her birth. A notebook, liquid ink and a fountain pen sat on a table to her right.

What was going on?

Her body trembled trying to come up with the reason she was taken against her will and she was coming up short.

One moment, she was in her home making coffee, flipping eggs over easy, and the next, she was snatched by two large men and thrown in a Mercedes Sprinter. If this was a kidnapping or rape, she wanted them to get it over with because the suspense was seconds away from causing her a heart attack.

And then the trees danced.

The leaves scattered around in space causing her heart to rock.

From her view she wasn't sure if a monster would reveal itself from the brush or not, because the massive windows made the scene look all the more horrifying.

As quickly as the leaves begin to dance, they stopped but she wasn't feeling any better. What was going on?

After what seemed like forever, the door opened. She heard one set of footsteps followed by another, another, and one more. She never had to count footsteps in her life. This was a first. But if she was accurate, she believed that there were four people in her presence.

“Can I…can I turn around?” She asked, swallowing the lump in her throat.

“You can if you want, but I must say, if you do, you will die.” The first man said. “Is that how you want to meet your last day?”

She shook her head slowly from left to right. “N…no. I…I don’t. What…what is your name?”

“We’ll get to that later. For now you can call me Number One, since I’m the first to speak. Everyone you hear after me, you may also assign a number. Although who we are, really doesn’t matter. But what you tell us does.”

“O…okay.”

“I know it doesn't seem this way,” Number One continued, “but this can actually be a celebration.”

She frowned, totally confused. “A…a celebration of what?”

“You won the project you bid for.”

She searched her mind and was coming up empty. Although she was sure that there was no project, not a single one that she would sign up for that would entail her being taken against her will, she was intrigued. “I think you have made a mistake. I'm not into anything kinky.”

Number One and the others chuckled.

"This is not for a kink."

"You not our type anyway, shawty," Number Two added.

"Just know that we have you here for a purpose," Number One continued. "And you did bid for a very lucrative contract. This gave us insight into your life. Who you are. Who you know. And so much more."

Now Sharon understood. "I know what you're talking about now. I was to be an in-house psychiatrist for a bank. The pay was too good to be true."

"Most things dangerous are."

"I was told I didn't get it."

"We lied," Number Three said, his voice somewhat younger but not any less confident.

She swallowed the lump in her throat. "What do you...what do you want from me?"

"Answers. To our questions."

"About psychology?"

"You can say that."

"You want me to help you with issues in your life?"

"You can say that too." Number One continued. "Now we must tell you our conditions."

"I'm...I'm listening."

"First, if you help us and do a good job, you will be returned safely to your home. A day later, you will be paid the original bid minus a pound of flesh."

Her eyes widened. "Sir, I—."

"Second, you will waste no time or delay because things will get worse quickly. And third, you must remain here for 48 hours."

She shook her head rapidly from left to right. "No...no, you don't understand. I can't stay here for 48 hours. I have a 15-year-old."

"We've made arrangements."

"For my child? How could –"

"We told you the contract you bid for was detailed. And as a result, we know everything about you. Just know that your son is with your mother. For now."

She trembled harder.

"Finally, you will keep everything you hear here confidential. If not, and we find out you have broken the agreement, we will pay you a visit along with a trip to your grave."

"Can I refuse the offer?"

"What do you think?" Number One said.

"We don't want you to be afraid," Number Three added. "Contrary to what you think we are great hosts.

As a matter of fact, you'll be given lunch, dinner, and breakfast in—."

"I don't mean any harm, but I don't want anything to fucking eat," she interrupted.

"It will be given to you all the same. Whether you choose to eat it is up to you. Because even though we have no problem slicing your fucking throat, we can still be gentleman about it."

"Why are you doing it like this?" She questioned. "There has to be a better way."

"We are one of the most powerful families in the world. You made yourself seen. We noticed. And now you must pay."

CHAPTER ONE

"I wish you were single."

Walid Wales sat on the stage of his strip club. From his view in the dimly lit place, he could see a state-of-the-art bar, a dance floor, and every other perk of the million-dollar facility he designed from the ground up. Suddenly, the lights dimmed further, and a spotlight was cast upon him in the center of the floor.

Garbed in a suit, an opulent tapestry of black on black, with a subtle floral pattern that seemed to drift over the fabric like smoke over midnight waters, he looked fucking *good.* Each button on his jacket was a golden orb, a solitary beacon in the dim lighting. His trousers matched the jacket echoing his style to perfection.

As seconds passed, he grew excited, when the music pumped from the embedded speakers as he prepared himself for the show.

The first beauty to descend from the ceiling, in Cirque de Soleil style, was a brown-skinned cutie with long black hair that feathered as she twirled down. The second was chocolate-toned with goddess locks that resembled mermaid tentacles as she spun. The third, fourth, and fifth strippers were just as stunning, showcasing for their owner a routine that would be reserved for only the richest clientele.

This wasn't a Vegas show. It was rich nigga shit, as fat asses, small waists, and kissable titties were on the menu.

And that seat alone would run you twenty thousand just to get a view.

Once all the strippers were on the floor, they spun around him, twerked, making him feel as if he were part of a spectacular show. Their skin smelled of sweet oils, and their outfits sparkled every time the light hit them just right. Walid felt proud that this would be his new place, opening in just two days.

And then the music ended.

Men would come from miles around to be a part of this, he was certain.

"Nice job, ladies," he said, standing up and hugging each one of them with one arm. "Nobody has ever seen anything like this in their lives."

Amanda, who was from Africa and had chosen a more modern name so that people could pronounce it correctly, accepted a towel from one of the club's employees and dabbed at a small sheen of sweat covering her forehead.

"So, are we really going to open up in two days?"

"Of course," he flagged an employee in the back who immediately brought up a glass of Hennessy Paradis. One of the most expensive bottles in the franchise. "Why would you ask me that?" He took a large sip, his gold watch sparkled in the light.

"No reason." She looked down and back at him. "It's just that I'm so excited. And I want it to be real. Like, I've never worked at a club with health care and—."

"I've spent a lot of money on this business. It's been my focus all year. So, when I tell you we're going to open up, that's exactly what I mean."

She smiled. "I wish you were single."

Walid hugged her again, hopped off the stage and walked toward the bar, where Cynthia, a Dominican beauty was waiting. She was holding a clipboard and grinning as he moved her way. He had let his wild hair go untamed again. Black, curly locks bouncing as he moved. But somehow it worked for him.

She was the manager who reminded him so much of Aliyah, his son's mother, that he almost didn't hire her. But she had other qualities he enjoyed.

"It's really nice," she said. "The ballers are gonna love it."

"This place will be elite. So money or not if they aren't the right type—."

"They ain't getting in," she giggled. "I know. You've said it many times."

"Because it's true," he said looking into her eyes, before following the curves of her body moments after.

"Where you going?"

He looked at his watch. "It depends. On what you got planned for me."

She placed her clipboard down on the bar and led him to his office. A lush space fit for a king. Dipped in black and sleek gold furnishings she walked to his couch, hit a button and the bed unfurled.

In control, she removed his glass from his hand and placed it on the table. With a gentle shove, he fell on the bed, and she crawled on top of him. Ready for the ride, he placed his hands behind his head as she unfastened his pants.

He was already rock hard.

"Damn he pretty," she said taking his thickness in her hand. She worked it over and over, like dough until he hardened so much he throbbed. Lowering her head, she licked the left side, followed by the right. He smiled, knowing she was teasing and playing a game.

But Walid was used to getting his dick sucked so he could play as long as she wanted, knowing that it will all end the same. With his nut rolling down her tongue.

It was showtime.

Finally her mouth covered his stiffness. Her tongue twirled and whirled until he was feeling so good that he gently touched the sides of her head and led her slightly. Easily he pumped into her mouth hoping to catch the four corners of her jaws. It was better that way.

Firm.

Soft.

Hot.

A few seconds later he was no longer the gentleman.

Rougher, and harder he got until before she knew it, she was drinking every drop.

Breathing heavily, she grabbed a few tissues off his desk and cleaned him off. With her head on his chest she said, "Where do you go in your mind when you get rougher? I like it but—"

"If you like it what's the problem?" He breathed deeply. "Anyway I'm not thinking about nothing," he kissed her on the top of her head. "Just let it go."

He closed his eyes for a quick nap, with his twin brother Ace in his mind.

Walid pulled his red Porsche Panamera up in the circular driveway of the Wales and Louisville Estate. The mansion loomed before him, a testament to luxury and grandeur, with its imposing facade of stone and intricate wrought-iron gates that whispered tales of big money. On the sides, ivy crept upward, softening the stern look with green tendrils, while an array of meticulously landscaped gardens beckoned visitors toward the grand entrance.

Walking to his home, he was greeted by the butler, who took his jacket and stepped aside. "Mr. Wales."

"Casey," he responded while he took a moment to remove his shoes and slipped into his black Valentino slippers.

The foyer, a vision of elegance, with polished marble floors reflected the soft glow of the crystal chandeliers that hung overhead. The interior decorator played no games. Even the air was scented with the subtle fragrance of fresh flowers from the arrangements that adorned the mahogany console tables along each corridor at all times.

He was ready for bed but not weary.

Instead of going to his room, he decided to visit his son's mother, Aliyah. Although they were no longer together, he still cared for her deeply and financially. In the beginning he didn't want her. She had hurt him too much for him to go back, so he chose to remain on the outs. Had it not been for her holding a grudge about the knowledge he possessed, that he accidently killed her father, she would have been his wife. But they could never get back right.

He even recalled what he said to her when he rescued her from the troubles in Belize years ago:

"You're my son's mother. I just wanted to make sure that you understand that we aren't together. If you can get with that, you're more than welcome to stay with me in the mansion. In your own room. Not in my bed."

And so, in an effort to respect his wishes she gave him space. And then even more space until before long, she felt so comfortable in the silence that she settled into peace.

He couldn't say the same.

As he walked down the hallway, he heard her voice and wondered who she could be talking to at such a late hour. Instead of entering right away, he stood by the doorway but didn't hear much outside of light laughter.

Joy.

How dare that bitch be happy when with the exception of his club, his world was falling apart.

Consumed with jealousy, he made himself known.

Their eyes locked.

Why was she so fucking beautiful?

Under the warmth of the dim lamp, Aliyah sat on her bed, the phone cradled between her shoulder and ear. The moonlight spilled through the open window, casting a silvery glow on her luscious black hair and bronzed skin. The red Hollywood style robe she was wearing, feathery sleeves, fluttered with a life of their own, and the daring slit along its length showcased her sexy thigh.

"So, I have to go, but I'll call you back," Aliyah said to whoever was on the other end. "Is everything okay," she asked Walid.

Walid remained silent; his arms crossed over his chest.

"Walid...are you—."

"Where's our son?" He asked.

"He's in his room with his cousin," she replied.

The boys' room was actually adjoining hers, allowing her quick access. But there were two entrances. One through her private quarters and the other from the hallway, where the family and nanny could reach the children.

In other words, if he really wanted to see his son, all he had to do was go through the other entrance. But she knew what this was about.

Letting her know that he could access her at all times.

Roman, was two years younger than Baltimore but they still got on very well. Walid needed it that way because he made a promise to his brother, the day he took his own life, that he would raise them together. Baltimore was seven years old, and Roman five.

"Is something wrong?" She asked, curiosity lacing her tone.

Walid wanted so badly to ask who was on the other line, but his pride held him hostage. "Nothing's wrong. Just checking up on the boys," he lied.

So why you in here? She thought.

"The nanny put them down earlier." She stood up, and per usual every curve was in place. "How did everything go at your club?" She questioned, clasping hands before her. "Are you ready for opening night?"

He winked and walked away.

Her beauty outraged him and suddenly he had no energy for small talk. Besides, he wanted to keep her uneasy, unhappy, in the hopes that at some point, she would return to him, confessing her love on bended knees.

It didn't happen.

Instead, Ace killing himself flashed into his mind.

He shook his head to erase his thoughts.

It wasn't working.

So, before stopping at his room, he went to the bar to pour himself another drink. He had become somewhat of an alcoholic ever since witnessing his brother Ace's murder. And it didn't look like things would be changing any time soon.

The bar was a masterpiece of design. Polished and boasting an impressive collection of liquor that gleamed under the soft light, he loved it there. The mirror backdrop seemed to multiply the various brands with a luxurious ambiance.

As he poured a drink, he took a deep breath. Every time his brother came into his mind, he would shake his head and pour another, savoring every drop.

Walid, once a family favorite, was unravelling and only time would reveal how far he would descend to hell.

MORNING

This was the room in the house nobody entered, mainly because it was located on the lowest level where it was always cold, dark, and less welcoming. Moreover, since the maids were not scheduled to clean that level regularly, it possessed a light damp smell.

Yet, it was in this hot mess that Mason Louisville and Blakeslee Wales carved out their existence. Despite both of them having their own rooms in the upper levels. Instead of staying in much more glamourous situations, at night they would be downstairs, and in the daytime, they would mess up the sheets in their private rooms, in the hopes that the maids would believe they were there.

Guilt never let Mason rest.

As he lay in bed, face up, looking at the ceiling, he did what he always did, tried to think of ways to get rid of Blakeslee's ass. One way he considered was being honest with his best friend, Banks, by confessing that he had been involved with his daughter. But he quickly dismissed that idea because it would destroy their friendship which could also end in his own murder.

"What you thinking about?" Blakeslee asked, nestling up to him. The white t-shirt gown she wore caressed her cream-colored skin. Her hair pulled up in a messy bun.

"You know I hate when you do that." He scratched his salt and pepper beard and then adjusted his big dick in his boxers. Although he was up in age his brown face was free of all wrinkles, adding to his mystic and appeal. Like really...how old was he?

"Do what?"

"Ask me what's on my mind. The shit I allowed myself to get into with you doesn't give you full access to me."

"Mason, I don't want full access." She laid on her side and propped her head up with her palm. "I just want you to remember that I'm pregnant, and when you're unhappy, I'm sad." She rubbed her enlarged belly for drama. "And that makes our child sad too." She breathed deeply. "Call me crazy but I think everybody would be happy for us if we just give them a chance."

He turned his head to look at her. "Why you so dead set on having a romance? I'm not fucking interested. You shouldn't be either when you know what it can do to me. When you know what it could do to your father."

She sat up straight and pulled her legs in front of her. "I've made clear who I want. And as far as our arrangement, I have done everything you asked. I've kept our relationship a secret, I've minded my tongue when I wanted to speak out, even when members of this family chose to disrespect me."

"How?"

"By saying I'm a whore! By saying I don't know my child's father!" Her heart rate kicked up. "You have to keep your end of the deal by making me feel safe so that I can have this child in peace, and maybe even have the life we—"

"We will never have the life you want," he interrupted. "I keep telling you that shit!"

She trembled. "Careful, Mason. The house is big, but the walls are thin." She got up, walked to his side of the bed. He sat up too, his feet planted firmly on the cold floor. Grabbing his designer slippers, she placed his feet into them for warmth.

On her knees, she eased her hand into his boxers. She'd done this so much, that her caps were bruised and scratched from having to be on all fours.

But the woman knew how to suck a dick.

She was good.

Too good.

He was thickening and he hated that she had that much control. He wished she understood that it wasn't because of her that he played along. That really it was his own stupidity of believing that she was Banks as a woman, someone he would always love.

"What you doing?" He asked.

He was so stiff now it hurt. Without asking questions she placed him into her warm mouth and sucked him proper-like. And for a second, just one, he remembered why he moaned her name.

Nineteen-year-old Riot Wales stood in the warm shower, enveloped by streams of water from the luxurious heads that came from all directions. The setup was nothing short of opulent, designed to mimic the sensation of standing in a soothing tropical rain.

As the water caressed his frame, it also cascaded down his silky, long black hair. Over the years, Riot had grown into a very attractive young man. Yet, because his features could also be deemed pretty, he began to harbor resentment towards his own image, often despising himself.

After his shower, he stepped onto the heated floor, grabbed a fluffy warm towel from the rack and wrapped it around his body. He was shocked when he opened the door to find Patrick Louisville, Mason's grandchild who was also Riot's nemesis, along with Bolt Louisville, Mason's son, in his room.

Patrick, eighteen, was very muscular, and it was evident by his chiseled physique. Since sixteen-year-old Bolt was his gym partner, his body was a smaller version of his, but still fit.

“What y'all doing in my room?” Riot questioned, wrapping the towel tighter.

Patrick smiled, a menacing grin on his brown face. For a moment he looked back at Bolt, whose light skin reddened with embarrassment for everyone.

"I don't come in y'all room, so don't come in mine!" Riot's unease deepened when he noticed something hidden behind Patrick's back. "And what you hiding?"

"Just something to make you prettier than what you already are," Patrick taunted.

With that, Patrick and Bolt grabbed Riot and slammed a brown curly wig over his wet hair. Next, he shoved him down causing his towel to fall off and his legs to go flying in the air. His limp but big penis rested on his thigh.

Down on the floor, they both lowered their height and smeared red lipstick all over his mouth and cheeks so it would look like blush.

Riot did all he could to resist the assault by people he thought cared about him, but it was to no avail. With him painted up like a clown, they had won, humiliating him in the process. When they were done, Riot lay on the floor, whimpering, while Patrick and Bolt laughed hard.

"I don't know why you won't just come out," Patrick said staring down at him. "We all know who you really are. Faggy."

"Yeah, be a man!" Bolt said, doing all he could to add to the madness.

"Get out my room!" Riot yelled. "Now!"

Finally they bounced, leaving him an emotional wreck.

Banks lie on the bed as Zoa Hawk slid on top of his strap. Zoa, with her small breast, tiny waist and fat ass rose up and down as her palms planted firmly in his chest. The black Goddess locs dripped down her shoulders brushing his tatted-up pecs ever so often. Her chocolate skin glowing due to the morning sun filtering through the window. A descendent of Ghana, she had been in the country most of her life.

With both hands on her waist, he positioned her the right way. Having fucked many a woman in his day, he knew what he liked. He knew what he needed to cum and cum hard. So he moved her slightly to the left, and then to the right, like he was tightening the strings of a guitar.

Over and over he positioned and readjusted until she was *right there.*

Zoa, loving the way he made her body feel was so wet her liquid dripped down his shaft and onto the sheets below.

"Banks...don't, don't stop," she moaned biting her lip. "Don't...don't stop. You feel sooo good."

He pushed deeper, watching her tiny breasts bump up and down with each pump. Before long he could feel himself heating up, so he arranged her again and came so hard his heart pounded like a drum.

Luckily, he was unselfish. Because of his makeup, he was the kind of man who could put in the work longer due to maintaining his stiffness always.

When Zoa reached an orgasm, she fell into his chest. Her warm breast digging deeper every time she breathed into his body.

Coming down, Zoa rolled onto her back and smiled. "We are so good together."

Banks sat up on the edge of the bed and grabbed his cellphone. "I hear you."

"Banks, you know you enjoy me as much as I enjoy you."

"More." He continued to tap on his phone, swiping email after email.

Looking over his shoulder she sighed. "You know what you want won't come that easily."

He glanced to his right, then focused back on his phone. "How do you know what I want?"

Zoa, sat up, her goddess locs cascaded down her back. "You trying to put things together for your island," she stated. "I think I heard you say Sunset Haven. But your family doesn't want to leave. And if you press them, you will lose them. Forever."

He turned to her. "Don't overstep, Zoa."

"Don't be angry. You speak of the island sometimes in snippets, two or three words at a time. You don't provide details, but I care about you and so I pay attention to everything you say. Listen to your family." She placed a warm hand on his back. "If you want them to be safe, find another way."

Banks rose, grabbed his black robe with the crisp, contrasting white piping, and slipped it on. For a moment he observed his frame in the mirror, remnants of what she said in his mind. After all these years, Banks Wales refused to age anything but gracefully. His salt-and-pepper hair and the slight wrinkles added character, each line a testament to a tale from a billionaire's life.

He walked over to the bed, sat down, and placed a hand on her thigh. "Listen, beautiful, I may go at it the wrong way, but I always get what I want. My family will fall in line, willingly or unwillingly." He kissed her lips. "I know something else I want too."

She giggled. "Are you referring to me, Mr. Wales?"

He laughed. "Why don't you let me take care of you? You don't have to work at your salon."

"You mean my salons? I own many."

"All I'm saying is that I'm wealthy enough to give you the life of your dreams."

"So I can go missing? Or die?"

He glared.

"Every woman who chose you, who said yes, is no longer here. It's like this family purges the female entity which is replaced with toxic masculinity instead."

"You sound unwell!"

She sat up, facing him. "When you met me back in the day, pulled me out of the projects and exposed me to the luxurious life, I thought I was in heaven. Then, when you left for your first island, and took it all away, I wanted to die. Thought I did something wrong. Now I know God himself saved me."

"Then why are you here? If I'm such a monster!"

"Because I can't and will never resist you. But I won't be hurt again."

"It wasn't like—."

"What I learned from that," she interrupted softly, "was that I can never have a man take care of me again." She shoved him lightly. "I also realized I love the glamorous life too, so I had to get my shit in order." She giggled.

"I never forgot about you."

"I couldn't tell. Time for a man as busy as you moves in seconds, but for people left in your past, or in your memories, it feels like forever to us." She winked. "So I don't need you to take care of me, Banks. I'm here because I enjoy your company, and I hope you enjoy mine. And when we're done, we'll go our separate ways."

"You're deeper than me sometimes, that's what I like about you."

She kissed him passionately and jogged toward the shower. Her brown ass cheeks dipping and rising with each move. "Now, let me get clean! Your family will be waking up and you know they love my food!"

Wearing a white crushed velvet tracksuit, Zoa walked down the opulent long hallway to prepare breakfast. The Wales and Louisville family members were up and moving around.

"Hey, Zoa," Minnesota said, holding Sugar's hand. Despite Sugar being Blakeslee's daughter, she and Minnesota were practically mother, and child and Minnesota loved that little girl as if she were her own.

Zoa waved and continued. "Hey, ladies! On my way to make breakfast."

"Yayyy," Sugar cheered.

Zoa giggled and continued her trek.

She bent the corner. The place was so big it was as if she were walking through a hotel hallway. "What's up, Zoa? You getting ready to make breakfast right?" Spacey inquired rubbing his gut.

"You know it," she said cheerfully.

"I hope you make some of that Ghanaian food. American breakfast is boring as fuck around here."

"I had the menu updated yesterday when I realized you were still in town. Don't worry, I got you."

"And that's why I love you too," Spacey said.

Zoa continued down the hall, greeting everyone she saw.

She was such a fixture that one night at a dinner party they all realized a truth. She was the first woman that Banks dated that everybody in the Wales family liked unanimously. To be honest it was easy. There was nothing to dislike about her. She was sweet, always willing to lend a hand, and wanted nothing from a soul. She had her own money and helped everyone in the household with the most mundane chores or situations.

For instance, when Minnesota was looking for a curly wig, it was Zoa who made the call to secure the $700 unit. Another time, Spacey was after a new pair of signed sneakers released by LeBron James, and Zoa used her contacts to snag them—a feat not even Banks could manage. Zoa was the real deal, and everyone wanted her to stay around.

The reason?

When she was there, Banks was happy.

And if he was happy, he wasn't talking about leaving.

After preparing breakfast, Zoa set the table in the massive breakfast room, where light poured in through the large windows, illuminating the lavish spread of both traditional Ghanaian dishes and continental breakfast favorites.

One by one, the family members entered...Minnesota, Sugar, Spacey, Walid, followed by Patrick, Bolt, and eventually Riot, who sat with his head down. Mason, Blakeslee, Joey, and finally Banks came a little behind.

As everyone entered, Banks looked at them and smiled. They were too happy. Too much at peace. And long-term peace gave him unease. He wanted to discuss leaving, fearing something bad was coming. He even listed all the reasons they should go, but knew, just as Zoa said, that the family dreaded long conversations. So for now he would let them breathe.

Sipping orange juice, he glanced at Mason, his longest and most trusted friend and raised his glass.

"Brother," Mason said.

"Brother," Banks replied raising his glass higher.

Who the fuck were they trying to fool?

Their love story, quite bizarre, was the realest thing about them both.

Everyone understood their relationship went deeper than friendship, brotherhood, and even blood. But Blakeslee didn't give a fuck. So seeing the loving exchange, she rolled her eyes.

Luckily for her, no one caught that shit but Spacey. Who was glaring her way.

Embarrassed, she stuck out her tongue and ate a piece of toast.

"I have a question, did anybody see my wig?" Minnesota asked giving Sugar a spoon for her cereal.

"Mama don't say that," Sugar said.

Blakeslee tried to hide her shame at hearing her daughter call another woman mama yet again.

"Say what?"

"Wig."

"Wig is not a bad word, honey," Banks said, loving his grandchild.

"But I heard Patrick say peel your wig back to Riot," She said filling her mouth with food. "And it sounded mean."

"Stop snitching," Minnesota said. "Well?" She persisted looking at the family. "Anybody seen it?"

Patrick scooped up his potatoes. "Riot, didn't I see a wig in your room?"

Bolt laughed.

"Why would you see it in his room?" Spacey added, speaking up for his son.

"Yeah, did you put it there?" Mason questioned.

"No, G-pops." Patrick said under his breath.

Minnesota was annoyed, "If you see my wig give it back. Please and thank you."

Silence kept them for fifteen more minutes. Just utensils clinking, juice drinking and eating.

As everyone enjoyed their meal, Spacey noted the unusual silence. "So, what's going on? We normally talk more than this. I mean a wig mystery. That's all we got?"

At that point, Aliyah walked in with her son and Roman, all three taking their places next to Walid. The silence persisted as Aliyah served herself and the boys.

"Let me tell you what I see," Spacey started.

"Ain't nobody trying to hear from you," Joey said to his brother. "Leave it alone."

"Hear me out!"

"Spacey, please shut up," Minnesota said.

"Listen, we all love each other, but we don't trust each other to be vulnerable and honest. And until that happens, we're cursed."

"What that got to do with my wig?" Minnesota asked.

"Man, just eat your food," Joey added.

"Exactly," Minnesota chimed in.

Spacey raised his hands. "I'm calling it how I see it. Y'all go ahead and enjoy the great meal. But remember this conversation."

CHAPTER TWO

"You can have tonight. But I'm going to remember your face."

The front of the Moneyed Nightclub was flooded with anticipation under a velvet night sky, where stars blinged like distant disco lights. Expensive cars lined the street, their sleek forms and luxury badges glinting under the moon's soft glow, setting the scene for an event that promised to be a Wales extravagance.

Even though the doors were slated to open at midnight, a buzz of excitement filled the air as the press, famous rappers, and renowned business moguls and social media influencers gathered outside on the red carpet. This was no ordinary opening. It was poised to redefine the nightclub experience entirely. As the attendees mingled, their attention suddenly shifted upwards when they heard a noise in the sky.

Walid was at it again.

And per his normal, made a grand entrance. Landing his all-black helicopter on the roof, everyone cheered as it touched down. The doors opened and

Walid eased out, alongside his brother Spacey, his sister Minnesota, and his father Mason.

The crowd's excitement intensified.

They were donned in the finest, having been dressed by a top fashion designer.

Walid spent more money on his fit. He wore a blazer that was a carnival of geometric patterns, its vibrant stripes of royal blue, electric yellow, and ruby red zigzagging against a rich black backdrop. A pair of shades hid his eyes, just the way he preferred.

"Welcome to Moneyed Nightclub," Walid announced from the rooftop. "Thank you all for being here! Shall we begin?"

They approached a glass elevator shaft and the crowd erupted in cheers as they descended. A masterpiece, they sparkled inside. Walid had it installed on the far end of the club and made it bulletproof to ensure his safety, or the safety of his elite guests.

Upon reaching the ground, he walked to the front, expressing his gratitude to all who came. Cameras flashed. People cheered and everyone couldn't wait to see the house that a Wales built.

Just as he was about to signal his staff to open the doors, the police arrived from the left, casting a shadow over the festivities.

"What's going on?" Walid frowned, confusion and irritation mingling in his tone.

"What's going on is that you aren't opening tonight," the officer declared.

Walid shook his head in disbelief. "Hold up, what did you just say to me?"

As if Walid couldn't hear but could read lips he spoke slowly and said, "You are not going to open. There were several notices sent to you which you ignored."

"That's a fucking lie! I responded to all of my notices, months in advance!"

"What notices are you referring to?" Mason intervened, his presence both commanding and calming for his son.

"Who are you again?" The official asked, taken aback by Mason's authority.

"A very powerful man that you don't want to fuck with," Mason retorted, his confidence unshaken. "Now answer the fucking question."

The official, clearly nervous, held his ground. "I don't know the exacts, but I still have a job to do, and this club won't be opening tonight."

The crowd reacted with gasps and murmurs, only amplifying Walid's humiliation. As if to add insult to injury, the police cordoned off the entrance with tape, threatening to arrest anyone who dared to cross its path.

Walid who was on the verge of confronting the officer, his frustration exacerbated by alcohol, was shoved lightly by his father. "This is not how we do business," Mason said before looking at the officers. "Not anymore. Trust me, we will get answers though. And those who disrespect us will pay."

Taking a deep breath Walid paused and removed his glasses and addressed the official. "You can have tonight. But I'm going to remember your face."

With that, he addressed his guests and told them another time. Afterwards, he and his family returned to the helicopter and ascended into the night sky, leaving the scene behind.

THE NEXT MORNING

Mason had a long night. After having to console Walid to prevent his rage from bubbling over, now he had to deal with Blakeslee. Standing in the middle of the lower-level bedroom he was trying to keep it together. Arguments were not uncommon between them, but this one escalated quickly.

"I don't care what you want," he said firmly. "I'm not gonna keep going over this shit with you. We not together and I don't owe you nothing."

She was sobbing. "I have been walking around this house for the past couple of weeks alone," she countered. "You won't even take me out. And let's not even talk about my own family."

"This shit is getting boring."

"Do you know how many people spoke to me in the past few days, Mason? None. Not even my father."

"And that's my fault?"

"It's not that it's your fault. It's that you don't even fake like you care anymore. You continue to maintain an excellent relationship with Banks, but nobody sees me!"

"What is it that you asking?"

"I'm asking that you stand up, be a man, and tell my father that I'm pregnant with your child."

Mason looked at her and backed up slowly.

Suddenly he burst out into laughter, mostly from embarrassment, but it annoyed Blakeslee immensely.

"Bitch, let me make this clear, I will never claim you. If you can't handle it, that's on you not me." He pointed at her. "I'm going for a run then I'm going to my own room. No dick for you tonight. So don't expect me back."

He moved toward the door, his hand hovered over the knob. He turned around to speak but decided against it. The damage and the truth was already done.

An hour later, Mason had just finished his five-mile run when he entered the Wales and Louisville mansion. He was confused. Everyone was sitting in the opulent living room, adorned with white and gold, exuding an aura of sheer luxury and big money.

Breathing heavily, with his hands on his hips, he asked, "What's...what's going on?"

Minnesota, playing with Sugar, said, "I don't know. Blakeslee called this meeting." She gave him a knowing look, indicating she, along with Spacey, was aware of their secret.

"Do you have any idea what she's going to say, unc?" Spacey added.

Mason felt as if he had been dropped down an elevator shaft. "No...but...where's Banks?"

"He on his way."

"Where's Blakeslee?"

"I don't know," Spacey said, "but if I were you, I would find her. Now."

Feeling dizzy, Mason ran out of the living room and caught Blakeslee in her room just as she was exiting. "What you about to do?" He was stern but concerned. He walked up to her and backed her against the wall.

"You don't care, remember?" She said slyly.

"Blakeslee don't play with me. I told you what I wanted when we first kicked off. Telling the entire family like this is a violation. I mean, my kids out there!"

"Can you move out of my way?"

"Blakeslee, don't do it like this."

Sounding like a parrot again she said, "You don't care remember?" She walked around him.

He tried to grab her arm, but she ran. He rushed behind her, but she was so fast that she bumped into Banks. Now shit was awkward. With Banks on one side and Mason on the other, Blakeslee stood eerily in the middle.

"What's going on?" Banks looked at her and then Mason.

Mason gazed at her and then at his longtime friend. "I don't know."

"You good?" Banks asked Blakeslee.

She looked at Mason and then at him. "I'll tell you in the meeting."

"Well, I'm on my way too," Banks said. "Let's go."

They all walked to the living room, and Mason felt dizzy. This was really going down. Right here. Right now.

To make shit more intense, everyone was in attendance—Spacey, Minnesota, Sugar, Patrick, Riot, Bolt, the entire family, Joey included. Everyone except Aliyah and the boys.

Banks took his seat and looked at his daughter. "You got the floor. How do you want to use it?"

She looked at them all and said, "I have something to tell you, and I hope you don't take it the wrong way."

Spacey looked down. Minnesota covered her face with her hands.

"We're listening," Banks continued. "But why do I get the impression that you're trying to delay?"

She looked at Mason. "I don't feel like I'm a part of this family." She looked at the room. "And I want that to change. Now."

Banks nodded. "Okay, things are heavy, but I will admit I can do better." He looked at everyone. "We all can. Anything else?"

"No...that's it."

Mason let out an audible exhale, so loud that everyone noticed.

"You good, unc?" Joey asked, confused by the noise.

"He fine," Spacey jumped in on his hero shit.

"Yeah, leave folks alone." Minnesota added.

Mason nodded. "I'm...I'm good."

"You sure?" Banks asked.

"Yes, brother."

"I appreciate your attention to this, father," Blakeslee continued reminding everyone that it was about her. "Because if things don't start changing," she breathed deeply and stared directly into Mason's eyes, "I will be a problem around here."

Banks was lounging in a room adorned with mahogany and burgundy, an ambiance fit for a man of his stature. He was sipping on his whiskey when his friend walked into the room.

“Are you okay?” Banks inquired, his eyebrow raised in concern. “You looked like you saw a ghost earlier.”

“I'm fine, but I won't lie, I'm getting up in age, and so are you.” He joked. “It seems my body isn't handling things the same. That’s the noise you heard.” He nodded toward the expensive whiskey. “Pour me a glass?”

“Always,” Banks agreed, filling his cup, before settling into his recliner. Facing Mason, who took his seat across from him he said, “How you liking being back in the States?”

Mason hesitated and rubbed his neat beard. “At one point, I wanted nothing more than to be here, but—”

“But you're feeling just like me,” Banks interrupted. “You want out.”

"I mean, it's not like we aren't home, but it seems like every time we come, it's drama," Mason continued. "Drama that I'm starting to realize, the older I get, is not worth it."

"I heard about what happened to Walid. How's he taking it?"

"Bad. But I'm getting involved. Even had the official who came to the club punched in the face on his lunch break the next day and then fired."

Banks laughed. "You're worse than me."

"Yeah right." He sipped. "But I'll help him find out who's really responsible for the shutdown. Just hope it's not our sins coming back."

Banks sipped slowly. "Is there anything else on your mind, Mason? Anything at all? You can tell me. We created that bond since we were kids," Banks pressed. "Don't see a reason for it to change now."

"No," Mason said, a hint of suspicion in his voice. "Is there something you expect to hear from me?"

Silence was thick.

It filled the space between them, a barrier as hard and cold as ice. Mason downed the rest of his whiskey, stood up, and approached Banks.

"At some point, I want to spend time with you alone. We hardly ever catch up anymore. If you're not with Zoa—"

Oh, this is what's going on, Banks thought. "So, you got a problem with Zoa?"

"No, brother," he said honestly, a hand to his chest. "Everybody loves Zoa. I do too. Plus I want you happy."

For some reason Mason detected a flicker of disappointment in Banks' eyes. Did he want him to be mad?

"I'm just saying that as your friend, we haven't caught up, and I would like that very much."

Banks nodded. "I'll make sure I remedy that over the next few weeks."

"I hope so," Mason said before leaving.

Just as Banks was about to tidy up and prepare for an evening out with Zoa, Casey the butler, announced a visitor. "Sir, someone strange is at the door."

"Strange?" He put his glass down. "You didn't let him into my home, did you?"

"Of course not. He's still there and your security and gunmen are ensuring he remains peaceful."

"No doubt," Banks said. "Well...who is he? What did he say?"

"He said, and I quote, *I know where the bodies are buried.*"

Banks stood taller. "Send him in. And make sure my men remain ready. One on each side. And put one behind him, too."

"I'll add another for good measure."

"Indeed."

When the visitor, a man in a wrinkled blue suit entered. He looked both crusty and sneaky at the same damn time. And to add to his creepiness he attempted to touch Banks' whiskey.

Four guns clicked from behind, stopping his goal.

Slowly his hands raised, "I'm just thirsty, I'm just thirsty."

"Don't touch anything in my house, nigga. Don't move either," Banks warned. "Now, what the fuck do you want?"

"15 million," the man stated boldly.

"And how do you intend on getting that?"

"You're going to give it to me because I know a lot. About the bodies, the wars, the people you killed before you fled to a new country. I have names, dates, even audio from when you guys got too relaxed in your own home and said too much." He laughed. "You are a smart man. But please remember the walls are always listening."

"My patience is running thin."

"Like I said, you're going to give me the money. And happily too. And you're not going to bother to find out who I am. Because if you do, everything you love will be taken away. I can promise you that."

Banks dropped him. A hard fist to the mouth. It was so quick it stunned his men.

With a deep heavy breath he looked down and said, "Don't you ever, ever fucking threaten my family."

The side of the man's lip bled. "You hit me...can I have a glass now?" His eyes feasted on the whiskey again. A tongue lapped at the blood like a dog.

"No. But you can have an exit. Never return here again."

Banks men scooped him off the floor like trash. A gun to the back of his head.

When he was gone, he picked up the phone and said, "Mason, come now. We have trouble."

Pinera's Italian Restaurant was the epitome of exclusivity, catering only to the affluent. The entrance boasted doors dipped in gold, a clear indicator of its selectiveness about clientele. Patrick and Bolt Louisville approached first, their lineage synonymous with wealth, expecting nothing but top-tier service just for being born into money. Shiny chains draped their necks, and million-dollar watches donned their arms.

"What's your name?" The doorman inquired when they approached.

"Patrick Louisville, and this is Bolt Louisville," Patrick announced, a hint of arrogance in his voice. Bolt, though younger and normally not the type they'd allow inside, an exception would be made if his lineage was right.

"Let me see if we have space," the doorman said nonchalantly. He glanced down at his clipboard.

"Didn't you hear what I just said?" Patrick stepped closer, his embarrassment evident. "My name is Patrick Lou—"

"I heard what you said, nigga," the doorman cut in, "but I don't know you. And if I don't know you, you not getting in." He dropped his hand holding the clipboard.

Fuck him. He wasn't getting inside with that attitude.

At that moment, Riot Wales arrived, greeting his extended family with a puzzled look. Dressed in a white t-shirt and a soft pink tailored suit he embodied fashion and style all the way around the board. "Why y'all waiting out here?"

"He won't let us inside," Patrick said through clenched teeth. "Let's go someplace else."

"Nah, hold up."

Riot approached the doorman, who repeated his earlier question. "Who are you?" the doorman asked.

""The name's Riot Wales." Recognizing the name and face, the doorman instantly granted them entry, "Right this way, sir."

Patrick was pissed.

Bolt was psyched.

Now in the establishment, Patrick was a bundle of nerves, aware that while their surname commanded respect, it was the Wales name that truly held weight in these circles. This realization weighed on Patrick, highlighting differences between their family brands.

Seated at their table, Patrick and Bolt huddled together, whispering.

"Y'all good over there?" Riot said, tearing a piece of bread.

"Yeah, why wouldn't we be?" Patrick asked. "You got us in, on your big boy shit."

"Go 'head with all that. You should be lucky I even fuck with you since you did that shit in the—."

"You cried like a bitch," Patrick said, flexing his muscles through his soft black t-shirt. "I invited you here to apologize. So let it go."

"You know what, when you asked me to come out, I should've said nah." He grabbed his car keys and was preparing to hit it for the door.

"Wait...I'm just playing," Patrick said.

Riot glared.

"Chill, we family. We shouldn't be acting like this."

Riot remained seated.

And the evening proceeded smoothly until a young man, introduced as Butter, joined them, unsettling Riot with his close proximity. Wearing black slacks and a button-down long sleeve shirt, he sat unusually close. His lips were doused with gloss, causing them to shine.

The man was sitting for five minutes, when things took a strange turn. Patrick began snapping pictures, particularly of Riot with Butter, sparking an uncomfortable confrontation.

"Why you taking pictures of me?" Riot demanded.

"No reason," Patrick smirked ominously, leaving Riot in uneasy anticipation.

"I asked you a question!" Riot said standing up, over top of his head.

Patrick grabbed his fork and began pushing food around. Looking down he said, "Nigga, I will drop you if you don't get from up over me."

"Mr. Wales, is he bothering you?" The doorman from earlier asked Riot, eager to throw him out on his head.

Riot grinned. "I don't know, are you?"

"We fine," Patrick said to the guard.

"Is that true, sir?" He asked Riot, ignoring Patrick all together.

"We good for now," Riot announced. "But I want him gone," he said pointing to Butter.

Butter batted his eyes, licked his lips, and floated away.

After paying the check, as they prepared to leave, Patrick showed Riot a photo on Butter's social media, mischievously captioned to insinuate a relationship between Riot and Butter.

Riot was heated.

Once outside Riot, who felt gut punched, said, "What you...what you do that for?"

Patrick laughed. "Not what I did, what you did. I mean two pretty niggas sitting together looks like a relationship to me."

"I'm not gay! Why you bring him here like I am?" Riot's attempt to confront Patrick only led to laughter.

"White boy, what you do in your private time ain't got nothing to do with me."

"Nothing to do with us at all," Bolt added before they both walked away laughing.

Feeling defeated, Riot yelled out into the night.

In the heart of Hopkins University, the cafeteria was alive and buzzing. Voices and clattering trays created a stage of noise. At the center of it all sat Patrick, surrounded by his usual entourage. The spotlight of attention firmly on him, just like any other day. His charm was undeniable, his presence magnetic when he wanted to be.

"Yeah, blew my mind too," Patrick casually dropped the bomb about Riot being gay. "I mean if you go that way it ain't no biggie. You still my cousin. It just shocked me that's all." His eyes danced with sneakiness, knowing per usual he was kicking up shit.

Samantha, confused, leaned closer. "But ain't Riot your brother?" She asked, searching his face for clues. "I remember you saying that before."

Patrick laughed it off, a sound light and carefree. "He is but—."

"But why you here clowning your own people?"

The table fell into a charged silence, every pair of eyes flickering between the two. Samantha's gaze sharpened. "Well?"

"You still mad that I fucked and dumped you?"

"Whoa," one of the people said.

"Why you a liar, Patrick? You good for weaving tales. Are you doing it again for your last name?" Her voice carrying a weight that sliced through the hum of the cafeteria. "You hate yourself that much?"

Patrick's facade cracked. Embarrassment coloring his cheeks. "Lying about my last name. How you figure, bitch?"

"You a storyteller, Patrick." Samantha pressed on, her words a dagger to his ego. "And a bad one at that. Even your records make it clear that you a Louisville, not a Wales."

Patrick scrambled for his defense, his pride wounded. "And what's wrong with being a Louisville? Wealth runs in my blood, regardless."

"If that's true, why you lying?" Samantha's laugh was sharp.

"I don't have to lie about my—."

"My granddaddy know about y'all," she continued. "The Louisville's ain't nothing but a bunch of thugs and dealers from Baltimore. Now the Wales, now that's a name that ring bells. They got it from the mud. Built empires. But you, and your family, still ain't shit. So admit it, Patrick, you a fucking liar who hates your own people."

Rolling her eyes, she gathered her belongings and rose. Looking down at her friends she said, "Come on y'all. Let's find better company." Her companions nodded and left him alone.

Left to stew in his own bullshit, Patrick watched as his world shifted. Before now, they had always respected him because Wales or not, he still came from money. He couldn't even remember why he lied about being a Wales in the first place.

Now it didn't matter. He had gotten called out.

And then a girl walked up and sat next to him. A cute girl with long gold braids. Wanting to be seen and heard, she slammed her tray on the table. "You're going about this all the wrong way."

"Who are you?"

"My name is Marvel. And I'm gonna help you make this shit work."

He quit college the next day.

Mason was in the kitchen making himself something to eat when Patrick walked inside. "Hey, grandson, you want a ham sandwich?"

Patrick pulled a chair out. "Can I ask you something?"

"So it's no on the sandwich."

"Sorry, G-pops," he dragged a hand down his face. "I...I just—."

"What's going on?"

"Are we…I mean…when y'all grew up in Baltimore were you thugs?"

Mason grabbed a knife, another plate and put it on the table. Next, he grabbed his sandwich and cut it, putting half on the extra plate. "We had our good times, but we were known for trouble over everything else." He took a bite.

Patrick nodded, picked up his sandwich but didn't eat. "What about…what about the Wales'?"

Mason sat back. "What's this about?"

"I just want to know the difference in our names?"

Spacey entered and grabbed Patrick's sandwich from his hand, taking a bite. With his mouth opened he said, "The difference is y'all niggas hood and we royalty."

Patrick took a deep breath and stormed out.

"What's wrong with you?" Mason asked throwing his hands up in the air. "I was talking to my grandson, and you come in here on joke time?"

"Damn, my bad. I didn't know he was serious. The question dumb at best."

"True." Mason sighed.

"But if he can't take a joke, he gonna have a tough time surviving with us in adulthood." He bit the sandwich again. "This shit good as fuck, unc."

Mason and Banks sat on their patio looking upon the moon like a couple of wolves. Their butler had poured them two spiked cups of cappuccino per request and mood. Their security had just checked the mansion for recorders, and it was clear.

Now alone Banks said, "I'm gonna tell the family we have to leave again," he dragged a hand down his face. "I don't think the man's money request holds much weight but—."

"It could be real," Mason said taking a sip. "And you have a history of ignoring valid threats, thinking no one is crazy enough to fuck with you."

Banks nodded in agreement. "I take it seriously. I do. But I also know that no one is silly enough to fuck with my family."

Mason shrugged. "I don't see the difference but okay." Looking for a subject change since Banks was gonna do what Banks was gonna do, he said, "So, how are things with you and Zoa?"

"Steady. The way I like it."

"She putting pressure for something more serious yet?"

"Actually she's not." He nodded. "I don't know if it's a game, but if it is, it's working. Because I'm interested." He looked over at him. "How's your love life?"

"I don't have one," he cleared his throat.

"Nobody at all?"

"I'm single, brother," he said calmly. "I may fuck a lady or two, but for me it'll never go beyond that."

"Be careful," he nodded. "You know how these women are. If they don't get what they want, they can attack and draw blood."

CHAPTER THREE

"Leave it to you to play the whore."

Mason walked into Walid's room. He was on his fifth glass of Hennessy and looked spent. Lying face up on the bed, he turned his head when he saw his father enter.

"Hungry?" Mason leaned in the doorway.

"Nah...not really."

"We gonna find out what happened to your club. And who's responsible."

Walid sat up. "I know, pops." He took a larger sip.

"You ready to talk about Ace yet? Because everybody in this house has come to terms with it but you and Banks."

"I don't need no conversation about a nigga who off'd himself." He drank everything in his cup and poured another glass. "I'm good."

"If you don't want to talk to me, maybe you should talk to Aliyah. She—."

"I don't want to fucking talk to that bitch. About shit!"

Mason glared and walked closer. Walid immediately knew he overstepped boundaries. "You can burn, son. Let that shit get soaked out of your veins. I ain't got no beef with you because although I lost all my brothers, I didn't lose a twin. But if you ever talk to me like that again or interrupt me you gonna see another side."

"I'm sorry." He took a light sip. "Won't happen again."

"I'm sure when Ace took his own life, he did it so that you wouldn't be in pain. So you wouldn't have to do what you signed up for. Take his life and get rid of a problem for this family. But don't become him in the process, son." Mason left him alone.

Walid couldn't stop the pain.

Losing his twin hurt too fucking much.

Like literally, he saw his own face blow his brains out.

It was starting to consume him in ways he hadn't prepared for. Grabbing the liquor bottle, he turned it upside down and poured most down his throat and stormed out.

Aliyah lie on her bed, face up listening to music. She was on the phone after having a long day taking her son and Roman out to an amusement park. Wanting to get rest, she settled down in her nightgown on her bed when Walid barged in without knocking.

She sat up. Her heart rocked heavily because she saw the drunken look in his eyes. "I…I have to go," she said as she ended her call. "Walid, what you doing?"

"What do you mean what I'm doing?" He walked deeper into her room.

"You're invading my privacy. Regularly. And I don't like it."

"It's because of me you're even in this room. This is my family's house. And that means everything in this house belongs to me."

"So you want me to leave?" Aliyah questioned.

This was not his intention.

"I didn't say that. What I'm saying is, I can walk into any room I want in this house," he paced in place.

Something else was wrong. They weren't together but she knew the man since they were kids.

Taking a deep breath, Aliyah shifted the conversation. "Are you ready to talk about your brother, Walid? Is that why you came? If it is I'm here. I'll make myself available, baby. You just got to—"

"What you trying to say?" He challenged, visibly disturbed.

"I'm saying you've changed since your brother's suicide. You wouldn't have treated me like this before without reason. And if you think it's disrespectful for me to question your right to every room in this house, even mine, the issue lies with you." Tears rolled down her cheeks.

Why couldn't he open up?

Why was he so cold when he needed this woman more than air?

"You came here for something, Walid." She stepped closer. "What do you want from me?" Aliyah's tone was firm yet concerned.

Walid, feeling cornered, attempted to divert the conversation. "My club didn't open," he confessed, a rare admission of vulnerability.

"Why...why not?" Aliyah was genuinely surprised.

"I don't know. I made sure everything was by the book, but I was blindsided by some code violations shit. It feels like a fucking setup."

"Is there anything I can do to help?" Her offer was sincere, yet it irritated Walid's soul.

"No, I was just updating you on my situation."

"Okay, I—."

"Are you seeing some nigga, Aliyah?" His question, abrupt and unfair, caught her off guard. "Are you...do you got another nigga around my son?" He pointed at the floor.

"I have friends," she admitted cautiously, aware of his temper. "But no one has ever, ever, been around Baltimore."

He busted out laughing. "So, you're seeing multiple people?"

"Yes," she stood her ground, inciting his wrath further. "I...but it's not like you—."

"Leave it to you to play the whore," he said, his words cutting deep.

"Get out of my room right now!" Aliyah demanded.

He chuckled once more before exiting.

She fell on her knees crying.

While Mason was lounging, sipping his drink in peace, the atmosphere shifted as Minnesota and Spacey walked inside. Their expressions alone were enough to signal to him that his tranquility was about to be disturbed.

"What is it? Can a man not drink in peace?" He sighed, bracing for the inevitable.

"Not if that man is entangled with his best friend's daughter," Spacey laughed, getting straight to the point. "And my funky ass sister." He flopped on the sofa in the lounge. He wouldn't dare sit in Banks' chair.

Minnesota nodded in agreement, adding, "Exactly. I don't understand what you see in her anyway. She's my sister but she's gross as fuck. Neglectful towards her own daughter and everything."

Mason chuckled. "Why should you care about her being a mother? Sugar has you."

"She had every chance to be a mother to Sugar, and she opted out. It's not my fault that I'm the one she calls mom." She paused. "Now what are you gonna do about her? Because I've seen that look in her eyes. She's about to cause more problems."

Mason exhaled and took a long drink. "I'm at a loss with what to do about Blakeslee."

"What does she even want?" Minnesota pushed.

"She wants to make shit official. And she wants me to say she mine in front of all y'all niggas."

Spacey and Minnesota laughed loudly.

Mason chuckled too.

The shit was dumb, and everybody knew it but Blakeslee.

"If that happens, it'll spark a war within this family," Spacey remarked. "I hope you know that. We just catching our breath over Ace's ass. We not ready for another."

Mason glared.

"Not to mention father is using every excuse to ship us back out," Minnesota added. "Something I'm no longer willing to do."

"This mansion hasn't been the same since Blakeslee called that meeting," Spacey said. "And I know she not done."

"Y'all better get ready. Banks is set on leaving the US, and that's something everyone needs to accept. The fifteen-million-dollar threat sent him over the edge."

Spacey, curious, probed further, "So he is planning to buy another island?"

Mason waved off the speculation. "I'm not diving into his plans. Because for real he isn't even telling me. Just know, he's determined to bounce and he's building something." Finishing his whiskey, Mason stood, ready to leave.

"Whatever she wants, unc, you'd better find a way to give it to her," Spacey said. "I know it sounds crazy but the shit between y'all would cause a bigger problem than any threat we've faced before."

Mason strolled out to the garden behind the estate, where a sea of orange poppies bloomed vibrantly. In the midst of this floral spectacle stood Blakeslee, a wooden basket dangling from her arm as she delicately placed each flower she picked inside.

As Mason approached and stood beside her, she turned to him with a smile. "Aren't they beautiful?" She asked, her voice as soft as the breeze.

Silence.

"This is the prettiest flower on earth in my opinion. The richness of its color, the fragrance...To me, poppies symbolize everything I feel."

"How so?" He asked, not really giving a fuck either which way for real for real.

"I know some people prefer roses, but for me, it's always been poppies."

Mason, growing impatient with the direction of their conversation, interjected, “Blakeslee, what you want from me that I can actually give you? If it’s possible, I will.”

“Do you know why I like poppies so much?” She replied, ignoring his question.

This bitch was stupid.

His frustration mounted. He wanted to discuss the intricacies of their relationship, yet she chose to focus on the garden.

“I admire poppies because they require delicacy. If you aren't gentle, they wither and die upon being cut,” she explained, her gaze now locked on his. “And isn’t that such a waste?”

“How does this apply to you? Or me.”

“You extracted me from a situation that, I'll admit, was painful. My family never respected or liked me. All because my mother gave me my father’s dead name.”

He sighed, being aware of the truth.

“So I needed your kindness. But you, Mason, you're the most dangerous because you sold me hope,” she said, her voice laced with pain.

“I didn't sell you anything,” Mason countered. “That’s where you’re wrong. I always, always told you the truth. And that was, outside of sex, I didn't want anything more."

"Yes, you did sell me lies! You made me believe that it was finally my time, that someone could truly be there for me. And now, I'm realizing it was all a joke. Just like these beautiful flowers in my basket you won't be satisfied until I wither away and die."

Mason's frustration boiled over. "The thing that kills me, Blakeslee, is that we've had this conversation before. Nothing, absolutely nothing, will come between my relationship with—."

"Blah, blah, blah, my father."

"Exactly! A man I've known all my life," he stated emphatically. "And you don't understand," he added forcefully, "because if you did, you wouldn't put me in this fucked up predicament."

"Then why did you fuck me? Huh?"

Good point that caused him to go silent.

"What does he have that I don't have? Maybe I need to see his old ass pussy for myself and the—."

He slapped her and said, "You're selfish."

Her face burned but she liked it because his calm exterior was gone.

She glared at him. “I'm selfish because I offered my body, and you took it? You're the one being selfish for not loving me! For not at least trying!”

“That's how I know you never really understood our arrangement.”

“Rules are my kryptonite, Mason. You admired that about me from a distance, but now it's an issue.”

“What you saying?”

“Whatever happens next is your fault not mine.”

CHAPTER FOUR

"We have fun, but now you're crossing a line."

Nestled within the grandeur of the mansion Banks and Zoa were in the indoor pool house. A luxurious oasis, its tranquil waters reflected the opulent chandeliers that hung overhead. Surrounded by floor-to-ceiling windows it offered a view of the poppies in the garden.

Banks sat on the pool chair with Zoa on his lap, moving up and down slowly as they made love. She was so alluring he preferred to fuck her with the most light possible, just to see her beautiful chocolate skin and seductive eyes.

He had just pushed deeper into her, when she moaned so loudly, it rocked his heart. Falling into him, their bodies breathed heavily before settling down.

After collecting his items and putting things back in order, he pulled up his swim trunks. Next, he gazed at Zoa as they relaxed in the pool area.

Having had her back blown out, she eased back on her white two-piece bikini with her locs draping over her shoulders, giving her an almost ethereal appearance. “Why you looking at me like that, boy?” She teased.

He flashed a smile. “You know I'm a grown ass man.”

“I'm aware of who you are.” She laid on her side and nestled against his body. “Yet, you're still young at heart, aren’t you? Are you getting old on me already?”

He chuckled and gripped her tighter. “Never.”

“Did you make a decision on the extortion request?”

“I’m not paying.”

“I don’t think you should, but I don’t trust it either.”

“Like I’ve told everyone, it’ll be okay and I’m not budging on my plans.”

“What are they?”

“They remain private. Like I said, I will get my way though.” He looked down at her. “Enough with that. I want to talk about you.”

“What you want to know?” She rubbed his chest.

“Are you really gonna be gone to Africa for three weeks?”

“Banks, you know Ghana is my home, and I have responsibilities to—.”

"I know, I know," he interjected, "to take care of your family and friends. But you're in a relationship now."

She laughed, her eyes twinkling with understanding. "I'm starting to really get you."

"What's that supposed to mean?" He inquired, curiosity piqued.

"You want me not because you can't possess me, but because I resist being controlled," she observed.

His expression soured. "We have fun, but now you're crossing a line."

"I have figured you out. It doesn't mean I don't want to be a part of whatever game you're playing. But remember, games have more than one player. I'm your opponent," she declared firmly. "Not a pawn."

He chuckled, loving her brilliance. In fact it was why he kept her around. "So, you leaving for three weeks?"

"Yes, and I'm looking forward to it as well. I—."

Before she could finish, Mason appeared. "Banks, I need to talk to you."

"Of course." He rose, kissed Zoa goodbye, and followed Mason into their lounge. "Is everything okay?"

“Yes, but I want to grab a drink with you and tell you a few things.” He exhaled. “Before I do, did you learn anything more about the man who visited? The entire family pissed about the possibility of leaving.”

“I know,” he admitted. “They’ll get over it. I've got our best people on who the stranger is, but even they're moving slower than usual. Good help is hard to find nowadays. Our last Search Men would’ve solved the case in hours.”

“They slow on Walid’s case too. The more I dig the more I’m sure it’s not government officials who stopped his club from opening. Something else is happening.” They turned down the hall.

“Why does drama always follow us in the States?” Mason asked as they both walked into the lounge.

Banks poured whiskey for them both and they sat in their recliners, staring at each other per usual. “What is it, though? Why you yank me from my lady?”

“She’s your lady now?”

“The closest thing to it,” he sipped. “Now stop delaying. What’s on your mind?”

“I'm considering getting an apartment,” Mason revealed.

Banks placed his glass on the drink table and sat up. “An apartment. Why?”

"It's not what you think. I'll still be here most of the time. It'll just be for...personal use," Mason hinted, hiding the true reason behind his desire for privacy.

Banks sat back, trying to mask his disappointment. "I want you to be happy, brother. If you think an apartment is the answer, then you have my blessing."

The two shared a moment of reflection. "Trust me, this won't change a thing. I want you to know this."

"Then why you leaving?"

"I have my reasons."

"Fair enough, but I will miss you here."

"I'm not going anywhere," Mason reassured.

"We will always have a bond," Banks said. "This is the most important relationship in my life."

"I hope that remains true above all else."

"Hands up, white boy."

The restaurant was a far cry from Patrick's usual spots. Accustomed to the lap of luxury, he found himself in a filthy diner in a bad neighborhood. This was off-putting because unlike his Baltimore native grandfather, he was always accustomed to the best.

Seated across from Marvel, whom he'd met a little while ago at college, he was trying his best to figure out what she wanted and more importantly what she could do for him.

With a plate of everything in front of her she said, "I wanted to introduce myself formally because I been watching you and you been going about everything the wrong way."

"I don't know what you talking about."

She chuckled, leaning in. "First of all, if you want my help, we need to be honest with each other. Once we're transparent, we can move forward." She stuffed her mouth with pancakes and porkchops. "Because I want this venture to succeed for both of us."

"What venture?" Patrick inquired, clasping his hands on the table. "'Cause you still not saying shit."

She swallowed the food. Tapped a napkin in the corners of her mouth. "I'm a scammer," she confessed, a playful smirk dancing on her lips. "Well, that's not the label I choose for myself, but it's one I've come to accept because it don't stop my paper."

Patrick laughed and popped his collar. "Well it's obvious you don't know me. If you did you would know I got money. So ain't no need to scam people."

"But you do scam, and here's why," she countered. "First off, the Louisville name is trash in Maryland. I mean y'all got money no doubt, but the name don't hold weight. Like Gates. Bezos. Prophet. Wales."

His brows pulled closer together. "You should be careful around me. I could make you disappear."

"I know. That's the thrill of it," she said, her laughter filling the air, drawing attention from other customers.

"Are you crazy?"

"I don't think so."

As Patrick observed her, he noticed a wildness in her eyes, an unsettling yet captivating energy. "What you want from me?" He asked, drawn in despite himself. "I'm getting irritated."

"I want you to embrace your dark side, to fully dive into the Wales legacy, and to take me with you," she declared.

"Assuming I'm interested in whatever you're proposing, which I'm not, how could you possibly help me?" Patrick played along. "I mean look at where you got me. I don't move through places like this."

Her laughter grew louder. "I've spent my life getting what I want through my scams. I have everything from designer bags to the latest sneakers, but I'm not satisfied. It's time for me to level up, and that means..."

"Tell me quicker." He urged her to continue, intrigued despite himself.

"By becoming your wife," she finished boldly.

Patrick fell back. "Hold up...did you just say my wife?"

"You heard me. I'll pretend to be your wife, and you'll become the Wales you've always dreamed of being. I'll teach you what to say and how to say it. Because you may be rich, but you don't know what rich people like. You act like a hood nigga."

He got up. "So I see you tripping hard now. Let me bounce." He motioned to retrieve his wallet.

"The lesson starts today. Beginning with you not paying for this meal."

"We don't gotta do that. I can just use my card," Patrick reached in his pocket.

"No, let's make our exit without paying," she grabbed his hand, and pulled him out of the diner before he could pay.

As they ran out, with other customers watching, he stared at the weird woman. A sense of embarrassment washed over him, but he was also captivated. He felt alive.

Was it the Louisville in his blood?

He couldn't be sure.

Maybe there was something to be said for embracing one's darker side. Maybe time would tell.

Riot was in the gym, hitting the weights hard, the clinking of the metal echoing off the luxurious gym's walls. His muscles straining and slick with sweat in the light.

Looking to start shit, Patrick bopped in, his frame bulky in the doorway. "Let me spot you," he offered.

"I'm straight," Riot grunted, sitting up.

But Patrick wasn't asking, and with a flex, he forced Riot back onto the bench. "Hands up, white boy."

Riot, caught in Patrick's game, complied, his hands gripping the cold steel as Patrick slapped on more weight. Before Riot could even think to push back, the bar was soaring overhead. One wrong move and the weight could smash down, leaving more than just bruises behind.

Under the crushing load, Riot's arms shook violently, veins bulging as he fought to keep the bar off his neck and head. "Yo, get it off!" He yelled, panic lacing his voice.

The bar dipped dangerously close to Riot's throat when Banks burst in, his presence alone cutting through the tension like a knife.

With ease, he hoisted the weight with one hand, returning it to its rack with a clatter. "What the fuck is happening here?" He looked at Riot and then Patrick.

Patrick's heart sank, the desire to vanish overwhelming. This was the man he wanted to be like. His living idol. And he was looking bad. "We…we were just playing, and—"

"Playing?" Banks' voice was ice, his eyes locked onto Patrick. "Sounded like a man fighting for his life! That's how you treat your own people?"

Patrick stuttered, scrambling for an excuse. "I was—."

"I don't know what game you're playing, but I got my eyes on you." Turning to Riot, Banks asked, "You straight?"

His ego bruised, Riot stood, nodding. "I'm good, grandfather. I just need to step out for a sec." He ran out.

Head hung low, Patrick slunk away too.

Racing out of the gym Riot's heart pounded as he ran into his father in the hallway.

"What's going on?" Spacey asked.

With deep breaths he said, "Father, I gotta talk to you about Patrick."

"Okay, what happened?"

"He been messing with me since—."

"That's just boy shit," Spacey said waving the air. "His uncle used to fuck with me every day when we grew up together. He'll get bored when he gets a girl."

"But this feels evil. Mean."

"Look, Riot, that's just how brothers get down sometimes. You gotta learn to handle it. You pretty but you a Wales."

Riot was offended. What his looks have to do with anything? "But it's more than that, he—"

"Listen, Riot, you can handle Patrick. Do you hear me?"

At that moment, Riot felt a coldness settle in his chest. He'd come seeking a lifeline, only to have his plea for help cast aside. "Okay, father. I won't bring it up again."

"We gonna do weights later?"

"I guess," with a deep, shuddering breath, he turned and walked away.

Lila Montgomery, previously Lila Wales, meticulously prepared a wholesome meal for her children. She was excited to have all of her boys together under one roof. Her firstborn son, Riot and her twin boys, Rami, and Roland.

Lila came along way. Once a severely obese woman, which Spacey loved, she was confined to a bed for most of the days of her life. But after losing custody of her son to her ex-husband, she got healthy, lost the weight, and now rested comfortably at 170 pounds.

Riot alone was the motivation for the change. And despite not having him around due to him living in Belize, she treasured every moment they spent together when he was in town.

She wasn't the only one excited.

To Roland and Rami, Riot was an icon—wealthy, fashion-forward, and an early adopter of the first luxury car for every manufacturer. Then it was his generosity. Whenever they needed a coin, it was light weight for him to bless their accounts, with thousands at a time. More than anything, he spent time with them and showed them love.

He was the big brother of their dreams.

Their anticipation built up higher as they heard the soft strains of music from Riot's car.

Since he had three new vehicles, they couldn't wait to see what he was bringing.

"He's here! He's here!" Roland exclaimed, excitement bubbling over. "He got the new Tesla!"

After he parked, Rami mirrored his brother's excitement as Lila opened the door to welcome Riot, enveloping him in a hug that seemed to last an eternity. Since his return, their relationship deepened, built on a foundation of trust, honesty, and the unwavering fact that she was his mother.

She had always prayed he would come check on her when he needed a mother. And he had come giving her relief. Knowing men who were raised without one could be psychopaths.

It was time to eat.

Under the glow of the recess lighting, Lila plated up a feast fit for the kings. Thick, juicy steaks seared with a blend of spices, a heap of butter-laced mashed potatoes, and a side of seasoned greens. It wouldn't be complete without her buttermilk biscuits.

With her husband and her sons seated around her table, they indulged giving her multiple compliments in the process. Riot was used to eating food prepared by a chef, but there was nothing like eating cuisine cooked by his mama.

It was so good he walked up to her, planted a kiss on her cheek effectively melting her heart in the process. “It was great, ma. Thank you.”

“You’re welcome, son.”

His brothers teased them lovingly, and they all laughed with no ill will in the room. A far cry from the Wales and Louisville mansion, where he was the running joke.

After dinner, Rami and Roland retreated to their video games, leaving Lila and Riot to delve into more serious matters. Earlier she saw something. Faint bruises on Riot's face, causing her heart to sink with worry. “I know you're looking at my face, mama,” Riot acknowledged. “But I’m good.”

“I just want you safe,” she admitted. “But I understand if you're not ready to dive into the details.”

“I just don’t want you to worry.”

“Do you speak to your father?”

“I tried but, I don’t think he...something is off whenever I bring it up.”

“Your father will be there for you in ways he knows how. But the bond between the Wales and Louisville’s remain deep. Painful. Just give him time,” she encouraged gently, knowing all.

The conversation shifted.

"Oh, I forgot to tell you, your stepbrothers and stepsister are coming."

"I really can't stay, mama."

"Please! I promise you'll love them."

"What's my stepsister's name?"

"It's gonna sound silly. But her name is Susie Q."

Lila was right.

As soon as she arrived, there was an instant connection between her and Riot, despite her unconventional appearance. She was a pretty girl, but her hair wasn't kept as well as it could have been. She wore wigs, too close to her eyebrows and her clothing was cheap and unflattering. Her brown skin was also painted with way too much makeup which concealed her natural beauty.

But Riot didn't care.

She was a joy to be around.

She told him about her brothers, and how they were actors in a bunch of indie movies. He told her about his family and mentioned the name Wales whom she was already aware.

Conversation was light and easy and flew by. It was the best time he had with a stranger ever. After the getting to knows, Lila and her husband left the youngsters to themselves, allowing Riot and Susie to discover deeper shared interests.

Five minutes later, her brothers Dallas and CB entered. They both hugged her from the back and shook hands with Riot. Both of them had brown sugar colored skin and it was obvious they both worked out.

"Nice meeting you," Dallas said with a friendly handshake.

"Yeah, make sure it's not the last. And if you ever need actors, think of us," CB said jokingly. "We teach boxing too."

They both disappeared in the back to keep time with their father and stepmother.

Sitting on the sofa Riot had a plan. Just like her brothers, he loved her look, her confidence and felt for what he had in mind, she would be perfect. "I want to say something to you but...I don't know how you'll handle it," Riot said.

"Wait...I have to say something to you first." She seemed sad. "You saw me on Only Fans didn't you?"

Riot was thrown off. Leaning forward he said, "Did you...did you say Only Fans?"

"Yeah, wasn't that what you were gonna say? Because most people recognize me from there."

"Nah, I was gonna ask you something else. I have a proposition for you and your brothers."

"Me and my brothers? I'm listening."

"You said they're actors, right?"

She nodded.

"So, I want to hire y'all for my cast."

CHAPTER SIX

"If I'm given the order, I'm going to love taking a family member's life."

Walid strolled into the conference room within the mansion, accompanied by three men, each one prepared for conflict. Finally Mason and Banks had answers for their son. It was going to be revealed who was responsible for the early closure of his dream nightclub.

The family lawyer, taken aback by the presence of his companions, watched as Walid, embodying the confidence befitting a billionaire's heir, seated himself directly across from him.

A moment later, a detective joined the meeting, opting to sit closer to Walid.

"What do you have for me?" Walid asked the detective, eager to get to the matter at hand.

The detective slid over a manilla folder. "It wasn't just regulatory issues that kept your nightclub from opening. The obstacle came from two men. Two dangerous men. Brothers."

"Brothers? I haven't been around long enough to make enemies," Walid remarked.

“Sir, you're a Wales. Your family has a complex history in the States,” the lawyer said.

“And the challenges you're facing could well be an inheritance of that legacy,” the detective added.

Intrigued, Walid leaned back, signaling for the detective to continue. “I need more about their backgrounds.”

“These men are drug dealers who own a series of nightclubs across D.C., Maryland, and Virginia. They see the innovative features of your club, like the external elevator and the rooftop helicopter pad, as a threat to their more meager operations.”

Walid was seething. “What else have you found?”

“You also requested the names of these individuals’ connections,” the detective interjected. “I've got all that for you. Their girlfriends, sneaky links as you would say, and one of their wives.”

Walid opened the folder and briefly scanned the documents inside. A smile formed on his lips as he realized the extent of the challenge before him. “They fucked with the wrong person. They didn’t know. But they're about to find out. Their names?”

“Trent and Cooper Falcon.”

The night was adorned with stars, yet Mason's focus was solely on the road ahead as he drove Blakeslee to a secret destination. She was radiant in a black dress that accentuated her pregnancy.

Mason, ever the epitome of style, donned designer black slacks and a matching button-down shirt, a small gold chain glistening on his neck.

"I can't believe you're taking me on a drive," Blakeslee marveled. "I mean we hardly ever go anywhere."

Mason chuckled softly, "Believe it."

"You don't understand how much I've looked forward to moments like this."

"Blakeslee, I know exactly what you've been waiting for. You never had a problem explaining yourself," Mason said, his words tinged with sarcasm.

She looked over at him. "Why does every word from you feel laced with hate for me? Am I that bad?"

"I'd be lying if I said I wasn't pissed with you. You're creating a situation I never wanted."

"You not a victim. I'm giving you what my father couldn't...my body, my womb. My eagerness to please you when he never gave a fuck. How can you resent me for that?" She replied, his tone softening.

"This isn't about resentment. It's about the pressure you apply. But let's not dwell on that tonight," Mason decided, aiming to steer the conversation away.

Blakeslee laughed, "If you don't want to talk about it, you sure have a funny way of showing it."

"Tonight, you have something else to celebrate."

"Me huh? Alone. This should be interesting."

Their journey led them to a wealthy suburb in Georgetown, where Mason's Aston Martin veered into a lavish apartment building estate. After nodding to the guards and parking with a view of the water, Blakeslee's curiosity peaked, "Where are we, Mason?" They exited the car and walked up to a secured door. "Mason, what's going on?"

"Let's not get loaded down with questions," he entered a code swiftly opening the door. And once they were inside, he escorted her through to a massive entrance, four stories high. Inside, Blakeslee's eyes widened in amazement as she realized his intentions.

"Oh my God, Mason, you didn't," she gasped. "Our very own place!"

"I thought about what you wanted. This apartment is our chance to see if we can go deeper." He led her through the stunning property to the top-floor bedroom, offering a breathtaking view of the water and city lights. "And I hope you like it."

"That's an understatement." Blakeslee, touched by the gesture, placed a hand on her belly, "This will make me so fucking happy."

He wanted to throw up. "Is that so?"

Suddenly she looked downward.

Sad.

Uneasy.

"Hold up," he said, "if you're happy, then what's the problem now?"

"Are you sure this isn't just a way to distance me from the house, from my father?"

"I do this for you and—."

"I don't mean to be ungrateful; I just want this to be real, more than I ever wanted anything in my whole life."

In the luxurious empty bedroom, Mason stood with the phone pressed against his ear. “Did she like it?” His friend River asked on the line.

He leaned against the wall and his jaw clenched. “Yeah. You picked a nice one. Almost too nice.”

“Don’t sound like you too happy though.”

“What do you think?”

She laughed. “How you gonna convince her to stay there forever, while you head back to the mansion? Because I don’t see it happening.”

Mason paced the length of the room, each step a heavy echo. “I don't know. But I’m gonna give it everything I got.”

“You can’t hurt her,” she said. “You know that right?”

In the dimly lit lounge, the glint of ice in the whiskey tumbler mirrored the coldness in Banks' eyes as he nestled in a leather armchair. The soft clink of crystal was interrupted by the buzz of his cell phone.

He answered.

"I'll need that money, Wales. You got seven days to cut the check."

Banks swirled the amber liquid in his glass, the calm in his voice hiding the storm brewing within. "Like I told you before, I'll be in touch when I'm ready. You don't rush me, nigga."

The caller's laughter burned his soul. "If I'm given the order, I'm going to love taking a family member's life."

"You won't get the pleasure."

"We'll see."

As Banks ended the call, his grip on the tumbler tightened, the anger boiling in him like a kettle. He stared into the depths of his drink, his thoughts dark and evil as he plotted the man's fate.

CHAPTER SEVEN

"We begin tomorrow night."

Banks and Mason found themselves in the depths of a dense forest, the light from their Escalade piercing through the trees, illuminating the area directly in front of them. Soon, a pickup truck arrived, its headlights casting beams in the opposite direction.

A tall, dark man with thick bifocal glasses emerged. Before he could approach Banks and Mason, he was thoroughly searched for any recording devices or weapons by their men.

Once cleared, Banks' armed guard signaled him to proceed, with Mason standing a few feet behind. "So I heard you came through for Walid."

"Yes, sir."

"I'm hoping you're here because you're doing the same for me." Banks stepped closer. "What do you have?"

"We haven't pinpointed his exact location, but we've narrowed down the vicinity," the man reported, his voice cautious.

"That's not good enough," Banks snapped. "I told you not to ring us until you were ready."

"I understand, sir, but I wanted to be forthright with you," the man replied. "And I think you may still be pleased."

"In which vicinity is he located?" Mason asked, his frustration evident.

"We believe he's in the Suitland Maryland area," the detective revealed.

"Suitland Maryland?" Banks echoed, perplexed. "I haven't interacted with anyone from that area in years."

"Doesn't mean they can't cause problems for you," the detective suggested.

Banks outlined their next steps. "Here's what we're going to do. I'll offer him the money, extend an invitation, and I want him followed and dealt with swiftly."

"I understand, sir," the detective confirmed. "When do we start?"

"We begin tomorrow night."

Giorgio entered the foyer of Banks' home, trailed closely by Banks' armed guards. As he stepped into the lounge where Banks and Mason were waiting, a sly smile spread across his face.

“I'm aware you had me followed. However, I assure you, even with your power, you have no idea who I am.”

“Your arrogance will be your downfall,” Mason interjected.

“Indeed,” Banks said.

“That may be true, but not within this lifetime,” Giorgio countered. “I'm among the rare few who've managed a life largely off the grid. No social media, no personal email or phone numbers. Shit, I only use a device for occasions such as this, leaving no trail of my existence. But I’m not telling you anything you don’t know as you also used face recognition software and came up short.” He laughed harder. “I must tell you, anonymity has proven to be a lucrative business.”

Banks scrutinized Giorgio's worn-out shoes, the frayed edges of his clothing, and the stained white t-shirt beneath his jacket.

Giorgio, noticing Banks' gaze, said, “You're probably wondering, with my wealth, why not invest in a better appearance?” His laughter revealed yellowed teeth.

"Yeah, why are you a nasty mothafucka?" Mason questioned.

"I relish the shock on faces like yours, rich men who believe they'll never have to engage with someone of my caliber. Proving you wrong brings me joy."

Banks approached the table where his whiskey resided and presented Giorgio with a document. "We'll transfer the funds to this account. After that, it's yours to do with as you please."

"Why not send it directly to the account I specified?" Giorgio questioned, observing the document.

"Because I don't want you having direct access to my resources," Banks said, with Mason chuckling at his friend's handling of the situation.

"Fair, but should the transfer fail, be prepared for the repercussions I promised, affecting your family and beyond," Giorgio warned.

"I'm not sure what you're plotting," Mason added, "but if you threaten my family in my presence again, I'll murder you without hesitation."

Giorgio's laughter broke the tension momentarily. "Perhaps I overstepped, but be aware, eliminating me won't end your troubles."

"But it will end mine," Banks added.

Eyeing the spot where the whiskey and paper had been, Giorgio asked, “May I have a drink now?”

“Fuck out my house, bum,” Banks flatly denied.

With a final laugh, Giorgio said, “Well, with the money in this account, I’ll buy my own bottle soon.” He exited the room, leaving an air of unresolved tension and funk behind.

Giorgio navigated the streets in his navy-blue Honda Accord, the interior reeking of cigarettes and unwashed leather. That wasn’t even the worst. The floors were matted in dirt and dog feces and yet the man didn’t care. He embraced this filthiness so much it felt like home.

Plus, he was in a good mood.

The money Banks promised was now transferred from the account Banks designated and into his boss’s registered account. Now he set off to meet his partner at a secret location, unaware of the helicopter discreetly tailing him from above until it was too late.

Despite his initial success in evading the helicopter's watchful eye, it reappeared, relentless in its pursuit. He had to shake him off. Close enough to his meeting point, Giorgio parked his car and ventured into the forest, seeking the cover of trees.

But the helicopter was gone.

Relief, until he spotted the drone.

Hovering above, larger than average, the drone kept a steady focus on him. "What is that?" He muttered to himself, puzzled, and alarmed by the drone's enormous size.

Fear replaced his usual confidence and arrogance as he realized the gravity of his situation. Desperate to shake off the drone, he zigzagged through the forest, but his efforts were in vain.

"Leave me alone!" He yelled, as if he was due mercy.

Out of shape, eventually, he found solace under a tree to catch his breath. But it was still there and there was no place else to run. Looking up at the drone with resignation he yelled, "Like I told you, after this, your troubles won't be over! Do you hear me? They're still coming!"

Moments later, the drone released a large object that landed a few feet from him. It resembled a shoebox.

"What the—."

BOOM!

It blew up in his face, turning his body into fragments. There would be nothing of him to recognize.

Giorgio the filthy was gone.

Seconds after the explosion, the money was rerouted back to its original account.

Back in their lounge, Banks and Mason observed the unfolding scene. While Mason felt a grim satisfaction with the outcome, Banks was unsatisfied, aware that Giorgio's network might be more extensive than anticipated.

“It worked,” Mason said with a smile. “All that yuck mouth and now look at his punk ass. Blood and dick on the ground against a tree.”

Banks continued to look at the scene through the drone’s camera. “This is not over.” He sighed. “Also, I don’t trust the detective. Something about him feels off.”

“Agreed.”

"I fired him already. I'll get better help for our next steps."

CHAPTER EIGHT

"If we gonna do this you not my stepbrother."

Riot navigated his truck, with Susie Q and her brothers, Dallas, and CB, nestled in the back. The plan was simple. They were going to be involved in his story, a movie of sorts. And because no one had ever seen them before, not even Spacey, in his mind it would work out smoothly.

Susie Q would act as his girlfriend.

And Dallas and CB would play his friends from college as well as his boxing coach.

As they transitioned from the city into a realm of lush greenery and secluded homes, where cries for help wouldn't carry from one property to the next do to being so far apart, Riot's guests were astounded by the change of scenery.

Upon seeing the massive homes, Susie Q glanced at her stepbrother in disbelief. "I can't believe you're living like this."

"What you mean?" Riot asked, genuinely puzzled by her reaction.

Their jaws collectively dropped. "Okay, you do know normal people don't live like this, right?" Susie Q pressed.

Riot hadn't really dwelled on it because it had always been his world.

He had always been cushioned by wealth and the notion of poverty was abstract, something known but not experienced in his life. As they approached the estate and he keyed in the code, the massive iron gates emblazoned with "Wales" swung open. Afterwards, he guided his truck through the extensive grounds.

"Maybe we aren't charging you enough," CB joked.

"Whatever your fee is I'll pay," Riot responded seriously.

"We playing but that's why we love you," Dallas added.

"And I can't believe your house is this far from the gate," Susie Q remarked still in awe as they continued to drive further. "This big time. Wow."

The moment they stopped, the butler swiftly opened his door and took the keys to have his vehicle parked. "Sir, Wales," Casey said.

"Hey, Casey," he smiled. "Follow me," he told the trio.

Once out of the vehicle, they walked through the large double doors. For the most part their heads remained on a swivel as they couldn't believe how high the ceilings were. Riot and his guests ventured down the opulent corridors, leaving Susie Q and her brothers in silent amazement. The grandeur they encountered was beyond anything they had imagined, challenging them to maintain composure and not fan boy out.

But it was hard.

Real hard.

Arriving at his room, Riot pushed open the double doors to reveal a space as large as an apartment. He invited them to make themselves comfortable on the couch while he casually removed his shoes and settled on the edge of the bed.

They were gagged. And yet Riot was so humble.

"Did you want anything to drink?" He offered.

"What do you have?" Susie Q inquired.

"Anything you want," Riot assured.

"For real?"

"Seriously, you can have anything you desire. Food too if you're hungry. If we don't have it, which we probably do, we'll send out for it."

"Beer?" Dallas said feeling crazy he didn't request more.

"Are you sure that's it?"

In the end they changed their orders, requesting lobster, shrimp, accompanied by cheese, crackers, and assorted snacks and drinks. When their treats began to arrive, they ate and enjoyed the food.

With their guts filled, Riot had other things in mind.

"Okay, now let's get down to business," Riot declared, ready to shift the conversation to more pressing matters. "My cousins, Patrick and Bolt, who are not actually blood, are fucking with me."

"Why?" Susie Q asked.

"They think I like men."

"And that's a reason to fuck with you?" Dallas asked.

"No but they think so."

"I don't believe it's because they think you're gay," Dallas remarked, casually sipping his beer.

"Well what do you think the real reason is?" Riot replied.

"Hear me out. I believe Patrick and Bolt are fucking with you because they perceive you as weak," Dallas clarified. “Saying you gay is just an excuse for them to be dumb. So trust me when I say that’s not it.”

Riot was at a loss. “All I know is that their actions have been turning my life upside down. And I need that to stop.”

“Why you don’t just let us drop ‘em?” Dallas asked holding up his fighting hands. “I’d break both of their fucking jaws.”

“Because it will make my father mad. I need it to be done a different way or my life will continue to be fucked up after y’all leave. This...this has to be lasting.”

“First off, you need to stop saying things like that,” Susie Q interjected firmly. “Your life not fucked up, boy. The moment you vocalize it, it solidifies. Let's just agree they've been trying to unsettle you, but we're here now, and we're going to ensure that shit stops.”

“I like the sound of that. So, based on what I said, what's the plan?” Riot inquired.

“The plan is for us to be seen with you more often,” Dallas explained. “Like you said, Susie Q will play your girlfriend, and we'll be your friends. Between that time we’ll teach you how to fight for real. But they don't need to know we're related. For this to work, we can't appear new. We need to seem like we've always been a part of your scene and they didn't notice."

"Okay, if that's gonna work we have to update your gear. Because everybody I roll with fly."

"What that mean?" CB asked, wanting to hear the words.

"It means it's shopping trip time."

All three of them grew excited.

"I like the sound of that!" Susie Q said.

The next day, Riot spent over one hundred thousand dollars on clothes for his crew. They had gear for going out. Gear for lounging, and he even made sure that Susie Q had every designer bag she wanted. Her favorite? Chanel. He also copped her a few expensive wigs to pull the looks together.

For the next five days, Susie Q and her siblings made their presence felt in the mansion. Whenever people gathered on the back deck, which was transformed into a resort-like oasis with palm trees, a swimming pool, a grill, and a wet bar, Riot and his people were there.

One particular afternoon, Susie Q, Dallas, and CB were dancing on the pool deck with Riot. With ass and cute titties for days, Susie Q was romping around with a red and green Gucci swimsuit and high heels, while her brothers were in red and black swim trunks.

Patrick and Bolt were also there, sitting in lawn chairs hawking from a far.

But something changed immediately.

Patrick's demeanor softened in their presence, a change that didn't escape Riot's gaze. If you a bully, be consistent. Why act differently depending on the company present? He thought.

When the sky darkened, Dallas approached Riot with a bold suggestion. "I'm about to say something out of line, and when I do, I want you to hit me in the face."

CB and Susie Q frowned, just as confused as Riot.

"Hit you. What you talking about?" Riot was taken aback.

"You heard me," Dallas affirmed, walking away.

"Just do what he says," Susie Q responded.

"It's gonna be fine," CB added.

As Susie Q cozied up to Riot, symbolizing her role as his girlfriend with a kiss on the lips and everything, Riot hesitated. His stiffness didn't go unnoticed. Whispering in his ear she said, "Nigga, don't play with me. If we gonna do this, you not my stepbrother. Now kiss me."

So he did. It was passionate as fuck too.

Even Spacey walking past the door caught the scene before he yelled, "I see you, son!"

When they were done CB noticed Riot was still too timid. Having been in many a movie he wanted more from him and his role. "Listen, if you want to project strength, this is how. Go off. Be cocky. Be strong. Dallas knows what he's doing."

He was right and so Riot nodded and waited. But what was Dallas gonna say to him to warrant a hit? The suspense was killing him.

After blending in seamlessly with CB and Susie Q, Dallas suddenly insulted Riot. "You a bitch." The Hennessy bottle turned upside down in his mouth, like he was drunk. Except Dallas barely had a drink all day.

Riot, recalling their plan, confronted Dallas. "Fuck you just say?"

"I said you a—."

Riot struck him squarely in the face, causing him to fall backwards. Next, he stood over top of him, breathing heavily. Blood poured from Dallas' lip. He went so hard that Patrick and Bolt were shocked, having never seen Riot react so assertively.

"Let me make this clear," Riot continued, popping his shit. "Disrespect me again, and you'll die."

"My bad, it won't happen again," Dallas played his part.

"It better not," Riot concluded, joining Susie Q and CB in the lawn chairs.

CB whispered, "I see you, Riot."

When Dallas got up, fake angrily, he winked at Riot out of Patrick and Bolt's view and smiled.

Patrick, accompanied by four of his friends, strode toward Verb nightclub, intent on enjoying the evening. He had carefully concealed from his grandfather the fact that he wasn't attending college, a secret he guarded closely knowing Mason didn't play with his education.

Although Banks had bequeathed Mason a significant portion of his wealth, ensuring none of his children would ever need to work a day in their lives, Mason aspired for them to possess intelligence and awareness.

In other words he didn't want them to be rich and dumb.

Yet, for Patrick, his own legacy felt like a burden. He yearned for the immediate gratification of being a Wales, tired of the struggles associated with his own name.

As they neared the club entrance, Patrick halted his friends. A bunch of mooching ass teenagers who enjoyed sponging off a billionaire's grandson. "Hey y'all, stand right here for a sec."

"Why?" One friend inquired.

"We going in, but I need to handle something quickly. Need to square things with the door staff," Patrick explained.

"Alright, we'll hang back, but make it quick," his friends agreed, lighting up cigarettes. "I'm trying to get fucked up."

Patrick approached the doormen. "Y'all letting people in?"

"Not right now. You'll have to post up like everyone else," the doorman replied, pointing towards a lengthy line Patrick hadn't noticed.

"I got cash though," Patrick whispered. "It's all yours if—."

"Any other time, I'd take it," the security guard admitted, "but we're under strict orders tonight. Being on the list is the only way in, especially with Oscar-nominated guests inside."

Desperation creeping in, Patrick played his last card, "Forget the cash. My name is Patrick Wales. And I hate for you to lose your job for not letting me inside."

The doorman eyed him skeptically. "I heard y'all were back in town but..."

"But what?"

"You're a Wales? Normally, they're... lighter."

He was heated. "I may not be light-skinned but I'm a Wales."

From the crowd, a familiar voice challenged his claim. "Boy, stop lying."

Turning, Patrick locked eyes with his nemesis, the same person who had called him out weeks earlier at the University. Samantha. And her presence spelled trouble.

"How 'bout you mind your fuckin' business. Ain't nobody even talking to you."

"So, you know him?" The doorman inquired.

"Yes, and that nigga is a Louisville. Don't let him in. He'll fuck around and tear up this club. Like his daddy did my grandfather's house when he owed him money back in the day."

The security guard's demeanor shifted, "Ah hell nah. You definitely not getting in now. We don't need nobody up in here fighting and shit."

Patrick's frustration mounted as the woman in line laughed. Embarrassed, Patrick rushed up to her, hit her in the mouth and watched her drop.

"Get the fuck out of here!" The security guard yelled at him.

"Now!"

"See what I'm saying," she said from the ground. "This nigga trouble."

CHAPTER NINE

"He shouldn't have access to your talent."

The bass was thumping, reverberating off the walls of Spirit Nightclub, where Trent and Cooper Falcon stood like kings surveying their domain. Dressed in slacks and crisp tees that did little to hide their street-honed physiques, their locs spread outrageously everywhere signaling a wildness like the command they have over the streets and their business.

They were sitting at the bar when one of the brothers noticed something. "Coop, you see what I'm seeing?" Trent's voice cut through the noise of the crowd.

Suddenly ten women and ten men in all black entered.

Cooper, a half-smile on his lips, nodded. "Looks like the night just got interesting."

In the lead, a woman with skin like twilight moved with grace, her eyes glinting with purpose as she approached the Falcon brothers. Stopping before them, she extended a small envelope, her gold nails catching the light.

"A gift," she said, her voice a melody amid the club's roar.

Both men, momentarily disarmed by her allure, looked at the envelope. Trent, his curiosity piqued, tore it open, his eyes scanning the contents. Moments later, the smile faded from his face.

The words said:
You wanted my attention, now you have it.

Cooper met his brother's gaze, the note's implication hanging heavy between them. "Who is this?"

"You should have stayed out of the way," she said.

Suddenly the men and women in black took bats to everything standing. They destroyed tables, the bar, the bottles. Cooper and Trent ran around and tried to stop the destruction. Guns waving, they didn't even know who to shoot.

The damage was so swift and outrageous all they could do was flop in chairs, and watch it go down. When the place looked like a demolition, with a swirl of her coat, she turned, leaving Trent and Cooper with the devastation.

While Brenda accompanied Walid in his helicopter, she couldn't help but feel as though she was living a dream. She was a plain jane, with light skin, a bun and a baggy dress that did nothing for her figure. This time he allowed his pilot to cruise through the night skies while he entertained. Walid, exuding the aura of a movie star, sparkled under the moonlight that illuminated their silver vessel.

She met him "coincidently" at Walmart when he claimed he was just stopping in to grab a few things. Unknowingly, the few things were her soul and heart. Clasping her hands in her lap, she sighed deeply, "I can't believe you chose me."

"Why you say that?" Walid inquired, turning to her.

"Nobody ever chooses me," she confessed, her voice tinged with disbelief.

"For starters, you might want to shift that mindset," he advised. "If you want somebody to give you more, you have to claim it first. Do you have a man?"

"I was wondering when you would ask."

He laughed. "Truthfully, it doesn't matter to me. Because I always get what I want."

She grinned. I'm kind of seeing someone, but..." Brenda hesitated.

"But what?"

"I've been with this guy for a while, and he only seems to want me when it's convenient for him," she explained. "Lately, since somebody keeps destroying him and his brother's businesses, he started taking it out on me."

"How?"

"Just mean...nasty. Hard to explain."

"You shouldn't accept that, beautiful. If he's taking his trouble out on you, it's not good for your soul," Walid continued as if he wasn't giving Aliyah the blues over at the Wales estate.

The pilot smoothly landed the helicopter on a helipad atop one of his luxury apartment buildings. And after they disembarked, Walid's team swiftly escorted them out of the aircraft and inside. Like every woman he encountered, Brenda was taken aback by the grandeur of the building. Once tucked inside, they entered a glass elevator and descended two levels which caused her heart to sink.

This place was epic.

Walid's fingertip pressed the pad and granted them access to a lavish apartment, its floor-to-ceiling windows, and luxury white furniture, screamed wealth.

“Have a seat,” Walid directed her to a plush sofa. Brenda sat, taking in her surroundings, as Walid played soft R&B music, setting the mood.

“What you drinking, sexy lady?” He asked, charming her with a nickname at the moment she didn’t deserve.

“Me...Sexy?”

“You don’t know you fine?”

She giggled. “I have never been fine in my life. I...I think the guy I was telling you about likes me this way. Because it wasn’t always the case.”

“I’m waiting for an answer,” he said.

“Oh...I’m sorry. Wine, please. Any kind you choose.”

Selecting a bottle of expensive Cabernet, Walid approached her, glass in hand. He sat so close she could smell his expensive cologne as well as the alcohol he’d been sipping hours earlier.

Somehow in his presence it made him smell sweeter.

“I have to be honest with you,” he began, capturing her attention with his extensive gaze and an arm around the back of the sofa. “If you going to be with me, I need you to cut ties with everyone else. Can you do that?”

“Cut ties? I mean...how do I know you won't play me?”

“You won't.”

“I don’t know, Walid. I'm scared,” she admitted.

“Of what?”

She looked down at her bare nail beds. “Being alone.”

“You'll never have to fear anything with me. But if you want the lifestyle I offer, I need absolute assurance that you're mine. I mean if you prefer the hardships of your past, that's your choice,” Walid stated, his tone serious. “But you have to decide right here, and right now. Because on everything I love I’m the realest nigga you’ll ever meet.”

Brenda considered her options; the luxurious lifestyle Walid was offering versus her current circumstances with a man who was growing meaner by the day.

Shit, the first time she met Trent at the grocery store he made her carry her own bags and his, as he claimed it was to get her number.

Finally, she made her choice, "I want this."

"Then prove it. Tell him you don't want him and cut him off cold."

"But I handle all of the accounts for his clubs."

He knew that, which is why he went after her first. "His problem not yours. If he doesn't want you, he shouldn't have access to your talent."

She nodded. "You're right."

"And remember, Brenda, don't lie to me. Someone might always be watching. It's best you stay on your best behavior if you want to be with me," Walid concluded.

"There is another thing I can do well. That he'll miss."

"What's that?"

"Let me show you."

She got on her knees, removed his dick, and sucked it with precision. No lie it was the best head he ever had in his life. And losing it he was certain, would cause his enemy to crumble even more.

A few days later, Brenda returned home after a shopping spree Walid organized. Her phone buzzed incessantly with calls from her ex-boyfriend, Trent who she broke up with days ago.

Fearful that Walid might have her phone tapped, she chose not to respond. This burned him up.

Just as she was about to shower, the sudden cessation of water caught her attention. Wrapping herself in a robe, she ventured into the living room, only to find Trent intruding into her space.

"What are you doing here?" She demanded.

"What you mean, 'What am I doing here,' woman?" Trent snapped. "Why haven't you been answering my calls?"

Brenda braced herself for a difficult conversation. "I have to tell you something. It's not going to work between us anymore."

"Not going to work! Are you insane?" Trent couldn't hide his embarrassment. She wasn't top tier. He only got her because she was smart. And now she was dumping him?

"That's exactly what I said," Brenda responded, her confidence growing. "You only want me when it's convenient for you. You disrespect me. Talk to me any kind of way. And I've realized I don't deserve that."

"So, what, you're cutting me off? What about my business?"

"Find somebody else."

He backed up and then laughed. She had done this before but always took him back. This was just like the other times. He just had to work a little harder. "Sure I got a few things going down. But I was gonna get right."

"It's over."

He nodded, tired of begging after one weak sentence of trying. "You know what, you gonna come running back."

"I'm serious this time. I need you to leave," Brenda walked toward the door.

Trent rushed towards her. "Can you at least kiss it before—."

"Leave, now!"

She was serious.

Pointing at her face he said, "Don't call me when whatever nigga gassing you up come to his senses.

Because I never liked your dry ass anyway. Orangutan face bitch," Trent yelled, storming out the door.

Walid sat in the bar with his father Banks in the mansion. He was sipping and feeling good, but Banks was seeing the destruction of his good son in real time, and it was tearing him apart.

"So you got at his girl, but what about Cooper's wife?"

Walid sat the glass down. "Nah, it won't work with her."

Banks frowned. "She ain't want you?"

"She's loyal for real," he chuckled. "But taking Brenda hurt them both because they don't know shit about running clubs. For now, I think I'm good."

"Never get comfortable."

"You right, father," he nodded. "But I will say something else, the more I think about it, the more I'm not sure if it was the brothers."

Banks sat back. "Why you say that?"

"They seemed legit confused on who was tearing them down. So if it ain't the Falcon brothers, who else is it?"

Banks nodded, concerned. "As always, we have to remain vigilant and apologize later. Because whether they responsible or not, if they got mixed in with you, they must've done something wrong on earth to deserve it."

Walid wanted to talk about something else. His brother Ace. "Father, do you ever think about—."

Banks got up abruptly and kissed his son on the head. It was a heavy kiss that was filled with pain. "Not now, son. Not now."

He stormed out.

And Walid knew he was just as fucked up as he was, if not more about Ace.

CHAPTER TEN

"This arrangement is not a fairytale for me."

Blakeslee twirled around the spacious living room of their new apartment, her eyes sparkling with excitement. The floor-to-ceiling windows flooded the space with light, making the gold and white accents of the luxury furniture gleam. Mason stood in the doorway, his expression unreadable, as Blakeslee enthusiastically pointed at a sleek, modern sofa.

Earlier in the day they were in the furniture store, and she was driving him crazy. "This one, Mason! It's perfect for this space, don't you think?" She beamed, her voice bubbling with excitement.

Mason glanced at it and sighed. "If you like it, get it," he said, his tone flat. "But let's not spend all day furniture shopping either."

As the day progressed, Blakeslee's joy in picking out furnishings contrasted sharply with Mason's detachment. He paid for everything, yet his impatience was evident.

Later that evening, the fully furnished apartment was filled with the aroma of dinner cooking. Blakeslee, donning a red apron, moved gracefully around the kitchen, humming a tune while she prepared their meal.

Not feeling like playing husband, Mason sat at the marble island, swirling a glass of wine, his demeanor still cold and distant.

He was so angry it was a wonder why he was even there.

"Almost ready." She breathed deeply. This is nice, isn't it? Our first dinner in the new place," she tried to lighten the mood as she placed two plates on the counter.

"It's food," Mason replied curtly, without looking up from his glass. "No need to celebrate every fucking thing."

Blakeslee's smile faltered. "I thought maybe we could enjoy this...together. Like a real couple. I mean can't you at least humor me?"

Mason finally looked at her, his gaze sharp. "Blakeslee, this arrangement is not a fairytale for me."

Her heart sank, but she refused to let the evening be ruined. "Well, I appreciate it anyway. I made your favorite. Spaghetti. I hope you like it."

He ate in silence, his mind seemingly elsewhere. As soon as he finished, he stood up, wiped his mouth, and placed his napkin on the counter. "I have to go. I'll be back in the morning."

Blakeslee's initial instinct was to protest hard and demand more from him. But as she looked around the luxurious apartment he provided, her heart broke, so she chose to be real. "You're always leaving," she said softly, more to herself than to him. "Always gone."

Mason paused at the door, not turning back. "I don't know what you expected. This the life you wanted. Me away from the family. So let it be."

With that, he left, leaving Blakeslee alone in luxury which felt more like a cage than a home. She wanted to argue, to tell him this wasn't what she desired. That being without him hurt more than death.

But she didn't.

As always, she sat in pain alone.

CHAPTER ELEVEN

"I'm tiring of this game."

Banks and Zoa were in the midst of a private moment when Mason, having observed them through a slightly ajar bedroom door, decided it was time to make his presence known with a knock.

"Who is it?" Banks called out, his voice laced with surprise.

"It's me, brother."

Zoa quickly covered herself, while Banks grabbed the sheet, pulling it up to his chest. "Come in," he said.

"You won't believe who's in the lounge right now." A hint of urgency in his tone.

"What you talking about?"

"You have to see for yourself," Mason insisted.

Fifteen minutes later, Banks and Mason found themselves seated comfortably in their recliners, staring down an unexpected visitor. Standing before them was Orlando. A big difference from Giorgio with his neat appearance, donning jogging pants and a matching jacket, his intentions were still far from friendly.

Banks' men had already ensured Orlando was unarmed, but that didn't diminish the threat he posed. "I'm here regarding the deal you struck with my partner," Orlando began, his voice steady.

Banks, unfazed, poured himself another glass of whiskey. "I'm not sure what deal you're referring to."

"Giorgio had his flaws, but he came bearing specific orders, orders that were supposed to be honored. Yet, the funds were returned," Orlando explained. "Why is that sir?"

Banks looked at Mason.

"Clarify your point," Mason demanded.

"I'm here for the $15 million. It needs to be deposited into a specified account, not the one you chose, which clearly granted you direct access to reverse the funds."

"And why would I comply now?" Banks challenged. "That's my fucking money, nigga."

"Because if you don't, things will escalate for you. I'm aware of the danger I'm in by confronting you but understand this...harming me won't end the plans set for you and your family," Orlando warned, his tone grave. "Just like they didn't go away when Giorgio was murdered."

Banks was furious. "I'm tiring of this game."

"This is anything but a game. And I know you know that, otherwise you would not have granted me an audience." He took a deep breath and readjusted his stance. "My mother once worked for you at Strong Curls."

Mason and Banks looked at one another.

"She spoke highly of you and how honorable you are. That's why, when your name came up on my list, I hesitated to get involved," Orlando shared, a trace of respect in his voice.

"And what made you reconsider?" Banks asked.

"Why does anyone change their mind? Fear, which was replaced with my need for money. To take care of my ailing daughter," Orlando confessed, his desperation clear.

Mason dragged hands down the sides of his face.

"Pay my boss. Let this end to keep your family safe. I'm begging you," Orlando pleaded. "Before I go, I want to leave a recording to let you know we're real. May I reach in my pocket?"

Banks nodded and his men aimed weapons his way just in case.

"Listen to this, and you'll know what's happening is serious." He placed a small recorder with a tape on his whiskey table.

When he left, they listened to the audio and was shocked at what was on it. Real-life times, places, and situations that only Banks and Mason were aware of. They even had their voices plotting crimes within the walls of previous US homes.

The threat was credible.

So credible it gave them chills. Not just in the States but any island they chose to roam.

Mason and Banks were forced to weigh the gravity of his request.

They were being outplayed.

Banks surveyed the room, where his family members were gathered for a crucial meeting. Mason, Walid, Blakeslee, Spacey, Minnesota, Patrick, Riot, Bolt, and Joey were all present, their attention fixed on him.

"I've called this meeting because we're facing a serious issue," Banks began. "We're being blackmailed again, and this time, the threat extends to all of you."

"So, we do what we always do, right? Eliminate the threat," Joey suggested confidently.

"Not this time," Mason interjected, his tone grave. "This person knows too much about our past, including where we live and our daily routines."

The young ones may have been clueless on the crimes of the past, but Spacey, Minnesota, Joey and Walid were aware.

Banks continued, "I could advise you all to lay low, avoid leaving the house, and keep a low profile, but I know better than to think I can impose such restrictions on you as adults. So we're bumping up security."

Patrick, Bolt and Riot sighed.

"Do we have any leads on who it could be?" Spacey asked, concern etching his features.

"Not at this time," Banks admitted, his frustration evident. "If I did, I might not be as worried. But rest assured, Mason and I are doing everything in our power to ensure our family's safety."

The suggestion that followed caused a stir among the family members. "With security being the short-term situation, long term, I believe it's best we leave this house," Banks proposed, a decision met with surprise and resistance. Quickly going over the plan, he listed everyone but Blakeslee.

And so, she was the first to voice her disapproval, misinterpreting Banks' suggestion as an attempt to roll out without her once again. "So, you're excluding me from your plans? As usual."

"Blakeslee, not calling you out was an oversight. I apologize. But if you prefer not to go, arrangements can be made. To my understanding from the younger ones, you haven't been around much anyway."

"What I tell y'all niggas about running your mouths?" Spacey asked.

"But I—."

"Don't make a small thing into something smaller," Banks interrupted Blakeslee.

The room grew tense as Blakeslee processed the implications of her affair with Mason.

"You know he means you too," Minnesota said. "Don't take it that way."

Walid cut into the conversation. "Father, I can meet you wherever you land but—."

"But what?" Banks said cutting him off.

"I have responsibilities here, and I can't leave until they're resolved."

"What about Baltimore and Roman?" Banks questioned. "They will have to go too."

"You're right. They are my priority, which is why I want to be sure this situation is done with my club before bouncing."

One by one, each family member echoed Walid's sentiment, unwilling to retreat.

Banks, acknowledging their stance, issued a final, stern warning. "While I respect your decisions, never forget who I am and what I'm capable of. If it means ensuring your safety, I will take whatever measures necessary. No matter how uncomfortable to you."

CHAPTER TWELVE

"If this wasn't the best day of my life, I don't know what is."

Riot's plan was unfolding better than expected. To his surprise, he found himself genuinely connecting with Suzie Q, who was originally cast as his faux girlfriend for appearances. After shaking security off, their bond deepened unexpectedly during a joyride, when he took her through the sprawling fields of a Maryland highway in his Benz.

With the sunroof open, Suzie Q stood, embracing the wind with her arms opened wide. It was both cool and warm at the same time and relaxed her soul. Settling back into her seat, she couldn't help but ask, "Where have you been all my life, Riot?"

His laughter was light. "I've been wondering the same," he admitted.

"Maybe we should make it official. And see what happens."

As the conversation steered towards the potential of something real between them, Riot felt compelled to uphold honesty. "I want to always be truthful with you. You're great, but you're not my type," he confessed, his gaze shifting away before returning to the road ahead.

"Understood. But...but can I ask you something?"

"Anything."

"Are you gay?" She inquired, seeking clarity. "I don't care if you are but—."

"No," he answered with a smile, reassuring her of his openness. "I'd tell you the truth if I were. I feel like I can be honest with you." He looked at the road. "I know I'm not the manliest person in the world. I got straight hair which I refuse to cut, and I like to dress neat and fly. But I like women."

She nodded. "I believe you."

Their drive continued in silence, Riot eased off the accelerator to observe the speed limit. When he saw her adjusting her wig which had shifted in the wind earlier, he said, "Let me do something for you," he suggested, sparking her curiosity.

"What?"

"Trust me."

Before she knew it, they arrived at Tyson's Corner in Virginia, a bastion of luxury shopping. Riot expertly guided her through a series of high-end stores, selecting a special outfit that flattered her figure while tailors took her measurements. Suzie Q was enveloped in a whirlwind of attention and luxury, and she was beyond grateful.

The transformation didn't end with clothes. After a visit to the salon, Suzie Q emerged with a black luscious sew in weave that cascaded down her back, enhancing her natural beauty and leaving her looking like a model straight out of a magazine.

"What's this all about?" She giggled, observing her image in a mirror. She felt like a goddess.

"Let me take you out. Like you deserve."

That evening, they dined on a rooftop, the cityscape stretching out before them. Suzie Q indulged in lobster while Riot opted for a chicken salad, the simplicity of his choice didn't take away from the taste.

Over dinner, Suzie Q grinned.

"What is it?" He asked.

"If this wasn't the best day of my life, I don't know what is."

He winked.

"I'm serious, Riot. You're an awesome person. And whatever happens after this, I want you to remember that," she said, her sincerity touching his heart. "Not just because of what you do for me, but how you make me feel. That's a real gift that not everyone possesses."

“I could say the same about you,” Riot complimented, the night air enveloping them in a gentle breeze. “And that’s why I like having you around.”

CHAPTER THIRTEEN

"We're upgrading everything about ourselves!"

When Patrick pulled up in his BMW in front of an old house, its windows nearly all broken, he hesitated, circling the property three times before deciding to stop.

Despite repeated calls where Marvel reassured him, "I live here. Where are you?" He finally braved the dilapidated exterior to follow her directions.

Stepping out of his vehicle, he made his way to a basement door, where upon knocking, Marvel quickly opened it wearing nothing but an oversized t-shirt. Confused, he noticed a video camera by the door, finding it odd given the building's decrepit state, thinking to himself that the place looked like it needed to be demolished. Not surveilled.

"You coming in, boy, or what?" Marvel called out.

Once inside, Patrick was taken aback by the cleanliness and modernity of Marvel's living space. A brand-new sofa, state-of-the-art television, and pristine appliances filled the room. The windows were intact, safeguarded by iron bars, and the air was fresh with a feminine scent, making him feel unexpectedly at ease.

"Okay, I'm here. So, what do you have in store for me?" He inquired, settling into the surprising comfort of the basement apartment.

"I have the scammer package for you," Marvel announced, guiding him to sit while her two fluffy white cats greeted him, one snuggling against his thigh, the other sitting at his feet, leaving their white fur on his clothes in the process.

"The Scammer's Package?" Patrick echoed, curious.

Marvel retrieved a toy box from the back before sitting beside him as the cats scurried away. Opening the box, she handed him an ID labeled "Patterson Wales."

"How did you...?" Patrick stammered, amazed. "This shit looks real!"

"I have my ways. You actually made it easy for me," Marvel confessed.

Patrick, puzzled, asked, "Why you say that?"

"You have a deceased relative named Patterson Louisville. He's not a Wales but he showed up with connections to the family," she revealed, tapping into forgotten family links to craft his new identity. "You didn't know that?"

Who was Patterson? He thought. He didn't know shit about his own people.

"Of course I do." He lied.

"Enough about that. Here's my identification," Marvel said, presenting her ID which read "Brandi Wales."

"You're calling yourself a Wales too?"

She dropped her hands.

In her opinion at this point he should get what she was creating. "If we're going to do this, we're going all the way," Marvel asserted, detailing their transformation plan. "We're upgrading everything about ourselves! Your wardrobe will shift from streetwear to designer suits, and I'll have my hair and makeup professionally done. Soon, we'll be the ones everyone wants at their parties."

Marvel's enthusiasm for their new lifestyle overshadowed Patrick's hesitance. "What you gonna do when we done?" He asked.

Silence.

"Marvel, what will you do?"

"Why would this be over?" She challenged.

"I mean, we can't live like this forever," Patrick reasoned. "It will only be for a little while. Because I got a life."

"It's just that...if it's good, let's not ruin it already. Let's wait and see and enjoy the moment," Marvel proposed, hopeful.

"I promise you this, I wouldn't be here if I wasn't all in. But it's not gonna be forever. I don't want you to think it's anything else."

Silence.

"Do you hear me?"

She grabbed a cat roughly and it screeched. "I hear you talking or whatever."

CHAPTER FOURTEEN

"I prefer you closer to home."

Banks was in his lounge for a serious discussion with Spacey and Mason. The pressing issue at hand was the unresolved $15 million transfer. Since he ignored the request, days had passed and the threats turned to pictures of his family members out and about, oblivious that they were followed or photographed.

And so he instructed everyone to stay home.

"What's our next move, pops?" Spacey questioned. "Because it's gonna be hard to get them to stay in forever. It's—."

"Why would it be?" He yelled. "We all know what's going on! Why can't my orders be followed?"

Spacey was quick to defend. "Listen, I've hardly stepped foot outside since you shared your concerns. It's Riot who's been less discreet, splitting his time between his girlfriend Suzie whatever her name is. And if he's not with her he's with his mother. I can't keep him away from her. He really likes it there."

"Lila?" Mason asked. "How's she doing?"

"Pretty good, I can't front," Spacey added. "She's healthier, happier and thinner."

Banks cleared his throat. "We're losing focus." He turned his attention to Mason. "And your family. Why aren't they laying low?"

"They've been doing pretty good. I've been misplacing their car keys to limit their outings, but that's a temporary fix. I'm in the streets just like you trying to find out who been extorting us. So until house security arrives, they can still slip out if they want."

"Security is coming but if they gonna be in the house I have to have them vetted. Extensively. Especially since I think it was a detail who recorded us last time. So it's taking a bit longer." He paused. "What about when you leave here? Are you being careful?" Banks took a sip.

"What you mean?"

"The apartment," Banks said firmer. "Is everything good?"

"Oh yeah, it serves its purpose for now, but I'm considering letting it go. In the meantime I been laying low."

"Good, because I prefer you closer to home," Banks expressed.

"Yeah, its best if you stay here," Spacey added. "Ain't shit popping off over there anyway I bet," he continued, referring loosely to Blakeslee.

"I'm gonna—."

"Mr. Banks, can we talk?" The meeting took an unexpected turn as Zoa entered. She never interrupted or called him Mr. Banks, so this was out of character. "You mind fellas?"

Spacey grinned, "Nah, anything for you."

"Exactly," Mason added as they excused themselves.

Zoa stepped up to Banks as if she chose violence. "So you actually tried to fuck up my trip to Africa? By messing up my connecting flight to New York?"

"I wouldn't call it sabotage," Banks said, his arms crossed over his chest.

"You caused me to miss my connecting flight, Banks," Zoa countered, frustration evident. "Messing up my arrangements. That makes me angry."

Banks, unfazed, stood by his action. "I wanted you here because I don't trust what's happening now. I told you that."

"Your drama is not mine."

"It doesn't stop me from worrying."

She looked down, took a deep breath, and moved closer. "Our love languages clash, yours being control and mine being freedom. But you can't outplay me every time," Zoa pointed out, just as Walid and Spacey reentered.

"Not now, fellas," Banks said.

"They're with me." Zoa said.

"I don't get it."

"Ready, Zoa?" Walid asked, signaling it was time to depart.

"Sure am."

"What's going on?" Banks frowned, dropping his arms.

"Your sons are getting me to New York to catch my next flight. Guess you didn't think this through, and despite yourself, raised real men. Who happen to be pilots."

He understood now.

"Fair enough." Banks, caught off guard by this development, called Zoa over for a final goodbye. Their kiss was a bittersweet acknowledgment of their complex relationship.

"Be careful." He told them all.

"Always," Walid assured, as they left Banks to his thoughts.

CHAPTER FIFTEEN

"She's as good as gone."

Walid was on a warpath, his vengeance targeted at the brothers who dared oppose his nightclub venture. His strategy was ruthless. Hit everybody. And so he did.

But they hadn't hit back.

Why?

After inflicting turmoil in his adversaries' lives, Walid returned home, seeking solace by playing with his son and nephew. Dealing with Roman was hard at times, because even though he was his twin's son, he could see Ace's mannerisms in everything he did, and it hurt.

After leaving the boys with the nanny, his next instinct was to seek out Aliyah, but her room was empty. Since he'd known her, she was never out that late.

Closing her door, he ran into his sister Minnesota in the hallway.

"What you doing snooping around Aliyah's room?" Minnesota inquired, her tone playful yet probing.

"Where is she?"

Minnesota's laughter echoed in the hallway, "You really don't know, do you?"

"What you talking about?"

"Aliyah's moved on. She's seeing someone who's feeling her hard," Minnesota revealed, her words hitting Walid like a ton of bricks.

"Seeing someone. You saw him?"

"She shared it with me."

His eyebrows raised. "How come you ain't tell me?"

"You said you didn't want her."

"But you still don't say nothing?" Walid's voice was filled with betrayal. "I'm your brother."

Minnesota's response was firm, "It's not my job to update you. It's your job to be present in the lives of those who matter to you. So, if you want the woman, you better fight for her. Because if not, she's as good as gone."

Walid paced in place. "Do you...do you know what kind of person he is?"

"He's an ambitious lawyer with a thriving career. The man been doing all he could to show her he wanted her, but she pushed back for a long time."

That shit hurt. "Why?"

"She loves you. But he kept confessing that he wanted to take care of her. So she decided to give him a try," she added before leaving him with a kiss on the cheek.

Left alone in the hallway, Walid was forced to confront the reality of his neglect, having no one to blame but himself.

Marvel had played her part flawlessly, ensuring that Patterson Wales became the talk of the town. He still acted like a hood nigga every now and again, but she worked on him, got out the kinks and embarrassed him lightly if he fell off. Before long, every hotspot desired their presence, a testament to how the right name could elevate one's status.

For the evening, despite Mason telling him to stay out the way and off the streets, Patrick and Marvel found themselves seated in an exclusive soul food restaurant, a new establishment hungry for the kind of publicity the Wales name could afford, on par with industry magnates and celebrities.

They had been in there for a minute having dinner when suddenly they were interrupted by a stunning woman approaching their table. Her beauty was so captivating it demanded a moment's pause before he could speak.

"Mr. Wales."

He loved the sound of that. "How can I help you?" He inquired, his tone polite yet cautious.

Marvel's gaze sharpened, a clear warning shot as the woman introduced herself.

"I just wanted to say it's a pleasure to meet you. I'm Lola. One of the owners."

"Lola," Patrick repeated, a smile playing on his lips, momentarily taken by her seduction.

Seeing him swell up, Marvel's glare intensified on him. They were supposed to be a united front, a couple, but Patrick wasn't playing his part.

"I don't want to interrupt your meal," Lola added.

"Then don't," Marvel snapped, her patience thinning.

Undeterred, Lola said, "Outside of this place, I also have a spa. It's called *Tickles* in Baltimore. We offer first class massages that I'm sure you would love." She handed him a card.

"I might have to check it out."

"Do that." With a final glance at Patrick, she departed, leaving an awkward silence in her wake.

She hadn't said a mumbling word to Marvel's ass.

Attempting to brush off the encounter, Patrick engaged Marvel in charity conversation, the flow of champagne momentarily easing the tension.

When it was time to leave, it was also time to do what they always did. Show affection in public, hoping a camera would catch the love affair. But the moment he reached for a hug, and pulled her into his body, he received an unexpected sharp bite to his shoulder.

"What you doing?" He exclaimed, shoving her into a table. "Fuck is wrong with you!"

She rushed forward and pointed in his face. "Don't ever disrespect me like that in public again," Marvel warned, her voice low but fierce. "If you do, I can do far worse I promise."

With that, she stormed off towards their car, leaving Patrick looking dumb.

Riot was in the throes of excitement, meticulously selecting a suit for an evening out with Suzy Q. She was supposed to be coming over but if he could escape first, so she wouldn't have to drive, he would do just that.

After showering and applying lotion to his skin, he styled his hair into a sleek man bun. As he dressed, the background music enhanced his mood, and he admired his reflection with a sense of satisfaction.

Just as he was about to leave, keys in hand, he encountered Patrick in the hallway. It was unfortunate for two reasons. First, Patrick had just experienced an argument with Marvel, and second, they were both wearing identical pale blue suits.

"So, you been raiding my closet now?" Patrick accused, stepping closer.

"Why would I do that?" Riot responded, genuinely puzzled by the accusation. "In your entire life you ain't never been fly as me."

Patrick's anger was visible, his frustrations boiling over not just from their wardrobe clash but from deeper issues related to identity within the Wales and Louisville families. And so, in a moment of anger, Patrick shoved Riot against the wall, and he hiccupped.

"You can never be me," Patrick declared, his anger masking his own insecurities. "Ever you bitch ass nigga!"

Wanting to do more, Patrick then reached for the tie holding Riot's man bun, yanking it free. Riot's hair cascaded down his shoulders, a blend of femininity and masculinity that defied Patrick's narrow view.

The confrontation escalated into a physical altercation until Spacey intervened, pulling them apart. "What's going on here?" He demanded, surveying the two with great concern.

Silence.

"Somebody tell me something!"

Patrick retreated to his room without a word, leaving Spacey seeking answers. Turning to Riot, he offered him a chance to talk, but Riot, filled with years of unaddressed gripes, doubted his father's ability to understand.

"Like you give a fuck!"

"What you just say?!"

"You don't care!" He huffed and puffed. "I don't know why you don't care but I know you don't."

"Son, I'm confused. Y'all are family. Why would you—."

"He's not my fucking family! He's a Louisville!"

"Fair enough, but can you at least tell me what's going on?"

"I've been trying to talk to you, but you've never really listened. Why start now?" Without waiting for a response, he stormed off, leaving the mansion and the pain behind.

"Fuck!"

CHAPTER SIXTEEN

"You are missing out on a lot if you choose not to marry again."

Mason was spending time with Vivian, a beautiful woman in her early forties. They were at a gala to raise money for young black filmmakers. Just being in her company made him feel lighter as they stood next to a high-top table and spoke. He realized this was what he was missing.

Grown, sexy conversation at the highest level.

"Mr. Louisville, you're going to have to tell me something," she said, a beautiful smile gracing her face. She was wearing a long, elegant red dress that dipped dangerously in the front, threatening to show her glistening titties. "Why are your eyes always on me?"

"Since when does a man have to tell a woman what she already knows?"

"And what's that?" Vivian said.

"That you're beautiful."

She smiled and took a sip of her wine. "Why do I feel like it's coming from someplace else? Are you lonely?"

The smile washed away. “A man like me could never be lonely.”

“If you're speaking about your wealth, you and I both know that's not true. There’ve been countless individuals who have been surrounded by people only to feel extreme loneliness.”

Now he wished he was entertaining a young dumb bitch. Because at least they wouldn’t be reading his mind. “You way off.”

“I don't care how rich you are, Mr. Louisville. Money does not equate to love. Never has and never will.”

“Why aren't you married?” Mason said, choosing to change the subject.

“I have my reasons. Why aren't you?”

“I was but I don't think I’ll ever get married again.”

She laughed.

“What's funny?”

“You are missing out on a lot if you choose not to marry again.”

“Why you say that?”

“Life is really about having someone who will always be in your corner. We aren't fit to be by ourselves, and the sooner people like you realize it, the better off you'll be.”

He had that person in his life, but it wasn't a woman. And yet he chose to fuck his daughter. "Are you trying to destroy my night?" He asked.

"Absolutely not," she placed her wine glass down. "As a matter of fact, come with me."

In the large dressing room Mason sat on a bench with a mirror directly behind. Slowly she walked up to him and placed one leg over his right and then left thigh. She pushed and prodded his dick, and before long he was stiff enough to enter her pussy.

No panties.

She was warm.

Graceful and sexy.

Wrapping his arms around her waist, he pushed once and twice and before long, exploded inside of her. It was much too quickly for his taste. He hadn't realized he was backed up until then. Sure Blakeslee could make him cum, but it felt automatic. Like a jerk off. Nothing close to sex. And yet he felt he could do more with Vivian.

"You felt nice," she said kissing his lips.

"Ready to go again?"

As Mason pulled his Aston Martin up to the moonlit driveway of the lavish apartment complex he shared with Blakeslee, he took a deep, weary breath, hoping against hope that she would be asleep. It was well past midnight, yet in his heart, he knew the universe didn't fuck with him or his sneaky ass ways.

Easing out the car, Mason walked with the light steps of a man bracing himself for the unknown. He took the elevator, a silent ascend to the top floor of their luxury apartment. And just as he'd predicted, the moment he opened the door, there she was.

Waiting.

Wearing a soft pink nightgown that hugged her pregnant form, she looked angelic.

"How was the event?" She asked, tenderly stroking her growing belly.

"It was nice. We raised a lot of money."

"Really! How much?" Curiosity sparkled in her eyes as he tossed his keys on the table by the door and walked over to the bar, seeking solace in a bottle.

"Enough to help quite a few young filmmakers." He paused, then turned to face her. "And why you asking so many questions? I didn't know you were into film."

"I'm not into film, but I'm into you. And I thought we were supposed to be laying low. Does Banks know about this little outing?"

"He's still your father. Put some respect on his name."

"Why? You don't." She folded her arms over her chest. "Now does he know?"

He grinned, despite himself. "How can I help you, Blakeslee? I'm tired and I want to get to bed. And it's obvious you have something on your heart. So, let's deal with it, once and for all."

She walked to the back, disappearing for what felt like an eternity. When she returned, her arms were hidden behind her back. "I want to say that you're everything to me," she began, her voice quivering with emotion.

"Blakeslee, please don't—"

"And I know you know that because I've made it clear." She said a bit louder. "But it's important for me to really express that to you."

Mason sighed. "What is this?"

When she finally revealed her hands, she held a gold ring box between them. “Mason, will you—.”

“What you doing?” He asked, his voice a hoarse whisper. “Don’t do this shit!”

She dropped to one knee. “Mason Louisville, I love you more than I've loved any man ever.”

“You hardly ever knew any men long enough to—”

“I haven't had many men stay with me, but I have had many men.”

“And you’re proud of this shit?”

“What is that supposed to mean?”

“Little girl, before we started messing around, flies were circling around your pussy. So quality was not something you were interested in.”

“So you’re saying that you’re the shit? A catch.”

“Yes.”

She grinned, her heart breaking. He was mean but she was used to it and wanted him all the same. “Like I said none of them, not a one, has made me feel like you.”

“Make this quicker.”

“Would you do me the honor of making me your wife and you my husband?”

“No.” The word fell between them like a guillotine, severing her head.

"Did you say no?" The smile melted.

"I said fuck no. Because I will not be your husband, Blakeslee. Not now, not ever."

She stood, clutching her belly as if to shield their unborn child from the pain of rejection.

"I don't know why you think this a game," he said, his voice cold and distant. "But I'm starting to think you're having a mental breakdown. It's almost like you say the same thing repeatedly and expect me to change my mind. It has never worked. And the sooner you realize that the better off we both will be."

"I'll tell my father and—."

He gripped her throat, pressing her frame against the large windows. If he pushed hard enough, who knew if the glass would hold her. "Threaten me again, and I will kill you!"

He released her throat and grabbed his keys.

Coughing she said, "Where...where are you going?"

He stormed out.

CHAPTER SEVENTEEN

"Since I don't know who it is, they have the upper hand."

Banks, Spacey, and Joey found themselves on the lush green of the golf course, the sun casting long shadows as they took their turns, a gentle breeze carrying the scent of fresh-cut grass and anticipation. It was Joey's turn first, and despite his best efforts, his shot went wide, missing the mark greatly. Spacey followed suit, his attempt faring no better, barely getting close.

Finally, it was Banks' turn. With a confident swing that spoke volumes of his experience, he hit the ball directly into the hole, a perfect shot that left his sons in awe.

Spacey and Joey couldn't help but laugh at their father's display of skill. "You love getting us out here just to show off, don't you?" Joey teased, the warmth of familial love evident in his voice.

"Farthest thing from the truth. When you're good, you're good. And it just showcases itself."

"Oh, that's what this is," Joey said, skepticism lacing his tone, while Spacey gave their father a serious look. "Because how we go from you telling us to stay in the house to being on the course?"

"Yeah, what's this about?" Spacey pressed. "Besides the ten men standing on the green who I know are armed, I thought this wasn't safe."

Banks took a moment before responding, the weight of his next words hanging heavy in the air. "I'm increasing security around everyone," he declared, his voice firm, leaving no room for debate. "In the next few days, in addition to detailed security when you leave, I'm also bringing guards in the house. I mentioned it before, but they passed the clearance an hour ago. And when they arrive, I'm instructing them to keep everyone inside."

"Not again, pops," Joey groaned, but Banks was resolute.

"I have to," he insisted. "The person is making more and more threats. Since I don't know who it is, they have the upper hand. So this is all I can do until some more info comes through."

Joey tried to lighten the mood, "I got a new girl I'm seeing," hoping to steer the conversation elsewhere. "This ain't good."

"She'll still be there when it's all said and done. If she's worth it."

Spacey shook his head, troubled. “I have no problem laying low, but something is going on between Riot and Patrick.”

Banks' expression darkened at the mention of the tension. “Going on. Like what? I saw a spat in the gym but didn’t know it was more.”

“It is. You know I try to stay out of the young boys’ business, but I don't like the temperature between them.”

“They always go at it,” Joey added, trying to dismiss his brother's worries.

“This felt angry,” Spacey countered, his tone serious. “So different, it has me keeping an eye on them.”

Banks, now fully engaged, saw the broader picture but didn’t give a fuck. “What does this have to do with my orders to stay out of the way?”

“Because if it's true that the boys are at war, staying in the house is the last thing they'll want to do.”

Their game of golf forgotten, the trio stood on the green, the tranquility of the moment overshadowed by the storm clouds of conflict brewing on the Wales and Louisville’s once again.

"Like I said, they'll be here next week. So they better get whatever they need to out of their system. Because we will be on lock down."

Banks found himself in the plushness of his lounge, a glass of rich amber whiskey in hand, as he engaged in his evening ritual—a phone call with Zoa. Their conversations had become a thread woven through the fabric of his daily life, and something he looked forward to.

"I miss you," Zoa confessed, "even though I don't know why I should, considering you try to sabotage my vacation."

"You're better than that," Banks responded smoothly, the ice clinking softly against his glass as he spoke. "Bringing up things that happened long ago is bad taste. Stay in the present. It will treat you better."

"So, how are things?" She asked softly. She felt bad for joking since his nerves were obviously rattled.

"Sir, there's a very important phone call," Casey said entering his lounge.

"Put it through."

"Right away, sir," he left.

"I have to go, Zoa. Later," Banks said, a note of urgency cutting short their connection. "Hello?" He answered the next call, bracing for what was to come.

"Sir, I begged you to pay the $15 million dollars. Why haven't you?" The voice on the other end demanded.

"I'm not going to be extorted anymore," Banks replied firmly, his stance unyielding.

"This isn't about extortion. This is about a debt."

Banks sat up straight. "A debt? What you talking about? I don't owe nobody shit. All my balances are at zero." The conversation took a darker turn, delving into a past Banks was unaware.

"I'm not supposed to be saying this but—."

"When I burn whoever is responsible down because I will, I will remember any information you provide. In other words, it's best to be on my good side."

The caller took a deep breath. "The twin boy. The one who isn't here anymore. He did something a while ago, and now it's time for you to pay."

"Are you talking about Ace?" Banks asked, a chill running down his spine as old ghosts resurfaced.

"I've said enough. Make this right. I'll be in contact soon." The call ended, leaving Banks consumed with fear.

Without hesitation, Banks made another call. One he hadn't anticipated making, due to wanting him to stay out of the gangster life for his own good. But now he felt compelled.

"It's been a long time," Banks began, the weight of years pressing down on his words.

"Wow. That's an understatement," came the response. "But I must say I'm happy to hear from you."

"We need to meet," Banks said.

"Anything you want, sir."

"I'll have a car sent to you."

"You know where I live?"

"I kept an eye on you from afar. How else do you think you got that job as head of security at the firm?"

He laughed. "I knew it was you. And now it's confirmed after so many years."

Banks laughed. "I'll see you soon."

When Banks laid eyes on Munro, the man who had once shielded him with unwavering loyalty before his departure to the islands, an unusual surge of optimism coursed through his veins.

The man was solid. Something not as common nowadays.

Munro, a steadfast guardian, had been there during one of Banks' most harrowing nights which also included saving his friend Mason from the clutches of his deranged ex-partner. Bolt's mother. And now, Munro was here again, ready to stand by his side.

However, the room held another figure from Banks' past, adding layers of complexity to the reunion.

Joanne.

Joanne, a friend whose history with Banks stretched back to a time when he was known as Blair, was also present. She sat across from Munro in the dimly lit boardroom. Their shared past was a tapestry of complicated emotions and unspoken bonds. At one point Joanne, harbored a crush on Blair, that was unrequited, but never absent of love.

Banks cared for her and always would.

Just not romantically.

The atmosphere in the boardroom was charged with anticipation, the soft glow of the lights casting shadows that seemed to accentuate the gravity of the moment.

"Okay, what do you need from me?" Munro broke the silence, his tone a blend of warmth and seriousness. "Whatever I can do, I will. I owe you everything."

"First off, it's good to see you," Banks began, the sincerity in his voice bridging the gap of time and distance. "Both of you."

"It's good to see you too," Joanne said. "Although, I am shocked that you decided to reach out."

"I have a situation," Banks continued, his tone shifting to one of urgency. "There's someone who is after my family, and now I have a good idea who it might be. I need it confirmed before I kill everybody."

The room seemed to hold its breath as he laid out the details. When things became clearer she said, "Like Munro whatever I can do I will, but what exactly do you need?"

"Using your unique skills online," he looked at Joanne, "and offline too, I need you to find the info based on what I provide."

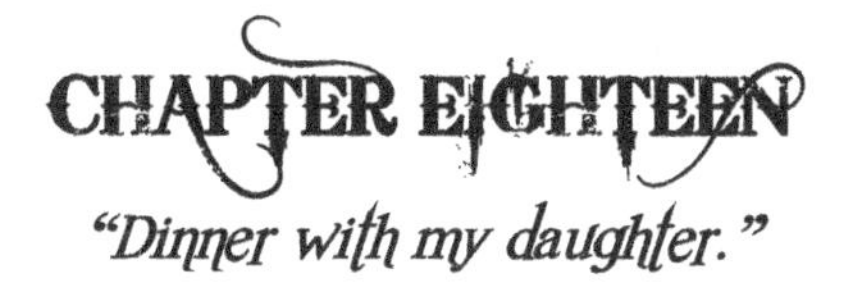

CHAPTER EIGHTEEN

"Dinner with my daughter."

Mason and Vivian were miles away from the comfort and complexity of their lives in Baltimore, cruising towards Virginia Beach. Mason, seeking an escape from the chaos, had silenced his phone, letting the calls from Blakeslee fall into the abyss of unanswered echoes. However, this time, as his phone erupted into a familiar melody, he answered.

It was Banks, which caused him some concern.

"Where you at?" Banks' voice danced through the speaker.

Mason, smiled at Vivian and focused back on the call. "I'm somewhere between here and there. With a beautiful distraction."

As he spoke, his hand found its way to Vivian's thigh and hers covered his, a warmth in the cool rush of their getaway.

Banks' laughter filtered through, "You off book and shaking security too. I thought we were laying low."

Mason nodded. "Yeah, I needed an escape."

"Not yet." Banks said. "Not yet. But right now, I've got news. It's about that extortion mess. Pick up the line."

Mason sent the call to his iPhone.

"I don't want to sound too sure, but I believe I know exactly who it might be."

As the conversation unfolded, Mason's eyes widened.

"And you won't believe this shit."

"Should I turn around?"

"No…trouble's gonna always be waiting. Just know that per usual, we might come out on top," Banks continued. "I'll give you details soon. I have somewhere to be too."

"So I'm not the only one." Mason nodded and melted a little deeper into the seats. "Where you headed?"

"Dinner with my daughter."

"So like I said, I'm not the only one," he said, putting a little pressure on the gas when he saw nothing but space. "It's two Wales members in the wind."

"Y'all niggas may be just using security, but you know I never move without them. So anywhere I go, protection follows."

Mason chuckled. "Well Minnesota should really enjoy the company."

"Nah. I'm taking Blakeslee out."

Blakeslee?

What the fuck!

The mention of Blakeslee, cast a shadow over Mason. His grip tightened around the steering wheel, the weight of his secrets about to let loose on his friendship. His heart raced at the thought of his world unraveling, of Blakeslee exposing the truths she promised to keep buried.

"You okay?" Vivian asked.

He forgot she was in the car. "Yes...I'm fine." Back on the call he said, "When...when?"

"Meeting her in three hours," Banks' words were heavy and started the clock in his mind. There was time to fuck shit up if he hurried. "Enjoy the ride with Vivian," Banks concluded, the call ending on a note that left Mason's thoughts spiraling.

With a sudden swerve, Mason's decision was made.

"Are you okay?" She asked. "Because you're really scaring me now."

"Everything's..." He started to lie but his night was ruined. "You know what, we gotta head back."

Vivian's concern was evident in her expression. Concern for him and disappointment for herself that she couldn't remain in the company of a billionaire gentleman for a little while longer. One that she liked a lot.

"Whatever you need," she offered, her support unwavering.

Quickly he made another call.

Blakeslee stood before the grand mirror in her bedroom. In the background a lavish array of perfume bottles were present, each a testament to luxury. To her right lay expensive makeup, alongside a hairbrush and comb, all crafted from pure gold. As she readied herself to hang out with her father, a shadow of guilt crept over her soul.

Because tonight she would reveal all to Banks, about her and his best friend.

With her hair styled to perfection and her makeup flawless, she stood up, her movements graceful. She was ready to slip on her soft pink dress, but the unexpected sound of the door opening caught her off guard, especially since Mason had informed her of his absence for the evening. Wrapped in confusion, she eased into her robe and ventured towards the source of the disturbance.

There, she was met by River, a figure who commanded attention. One she also knew from the past as Mason's hitwoman.

River, Mason's right hand Dom, stood over six feet tall. With tats over every inch of her light skinned body, she looked like moving art but to Blakeslee she was a living nightmare. Even her light brown locs added to her mystique and presence. Still, if she was there, it meant Mason was willing to do anything to keep her silent.

Now the owner of 17 Loc Bars in the DMV, she was an entrepreneur funded by the money Mason gifted her many years ago. But boss or not, she would do anything for the man.

Even kill.

Blakeslee faked a smile. "So, he found out, huh?" She murmured, already knowing the answer.

River stepped closer, her gaze intense. "What you doing? Mason takes care of you, provides for you, and this how you repay him?"

"How you gonna provide for a billionaire's daughter?"

"Let's keep it a buck, your father don't give a fuck about you."

Blakeslee's defense was weak against River. She knew the truth. "You don't understand the whole story," she attempted to explain.

"Loyalty, Blakeslee. It's a concept you must've forgotten. Or never learned."

The tension between them was concrete. "So, what now?"

River's response was firm, leaving no room for negotiation. "You about to call your father, claim you don't feel good and sit the fuck down. And you won't mention a word about me or Mason."

"And if I don't?"

"You might be unclear on where you stand with Mason. But don't underestimate the depth of our bond. Or what I will do for him." The threat in River's voice was clear, her loyalty to Mason unshaken by time or distance. "Now make the fucking call."

CHAPTER NINETEEN

"Come out with your hands up!"

Marvel had orchestrated the day for she and Patrick with precision. And he noticed something simmering, the façade was starting to be more about her than him. Every social engagement they would attend, would have Patrick playing the co-star in her world and today would be no different. After shaking Banks' security detail, the morning's agenda commenced with a breakfast and an assembly of new friends, where Patrick was amazed at how effortlessly Marvel put on the doting wife.

She was good too because he couldn't stand the bitch.

But she didn't seem to notice.

As they mingled, a distinguished black entrepreneur, known for his empire of Chinese restaurants across Washington D.C., complimented their bond, sparking a debate about how they met. Because no matter how good they put on, Patrick always felt weird to most people, and they didn't see the connection.

"How did you two meet?" He asked, his curiosity raised.

Caught in the web of their own making, Patrick stumbled for a moment before Marvel intervened. Her arm entwined with his she said, "Oh, like everyone does. Online."

And she proceeded with details that flew from her lips about a whirlwind romance that she painted in broad, vibrant strokes. With everyone who believed her, she seemed to get drunk with deceit.

This went on all day.

Transitioning from one event to the next even going to a baby shower hosted by a mogul in the beauty industry. The woman was also an advocate for women's rights, and so she was doing all she could to see if he was real. This followed by a barrage of questions.

"Don't you love her?" The pregnant woman said to him. "Because she rallies so hard for you. You should be kissing her feet."

Patrick squirmed under the weight of the conversations, feeling diminished by every room they visited.

As she spoke, a realization hit him hard.

He wanted out.

And he would get out. Soon.

The final stop, a charity picnic advocating for the acceptance of home births, pushed Patrick to his limits. He was so annoyed he stayed for five minutes and hit it for the door.

"What's wrong with you?" She asked rushing behind him.

"Listen, this shit ain't me."

"I know," she said rubbing his chest. "It's Patterson Wales. That's why—."

"If this is what being a Wales means to y'all, I don't want it. Fuck I look like kissing ass when I already got access to everything I want."

They walked to the car and was about to take off when suddenly police pulled up behind them. Patrick wanted to shit his pants.

"Fuck is this about?" She said, looking through the back window.

"I don't know. But they clearly here for us."

"Come out with your hands up!" An officer yelled aiming guns in their direction. The streets flooded with people asking questions and taking video.

"Now!"

Slowly they both complied, before lying face down on the ground. But when they took Marvel away in

handcuffs and he was told to go home, he couldn't believe his luck.

Driving down the road he realized he had gotten his wish.

Freedom from his suffocating fake wife.

Freedom from being Patterson Wales.

Riot was nestled in his bed, anticipating the embrace of his afternoon nap. A cherished ritual that had become the subject of family jokes.

"Pretty boy needs his beauty rest," Patrick and Bolt would say.

But Riot had grown indifferent to their teasing, especially with Patrick and Bolt making clear that his torment would always be their form of pleasure. So why try to impress them anymore?

Just as sleep was about to claim him, the butler's presence at his door snapped him back to reality. "Sir Wales!" The butler inquired, with a formal tone that screamed urgency.

"Yes!" Riot said popping up.

"Someone is here for you!"

"You didn't let them in, did you?" Riot's voice carried a hint of apprehension. "With everything—."

"Of course not, sir. I always verify before admitting any visitors," Casey reassured him.

"Well who did they claim to be?" Riot probed further.

"They claim to have met you through an app," the butler began, very embarrassed.

"An app? I haven't signed up for anything like that." He cleared his throat. "I have a girlfriend."

"It's not a woman, sir," the butler responded, sensing Riot's confusion deepening.

"A man?" Riot's frown was almost audible in his voice. "Send them away. I don't feel like any games. Patrick is probably involved as usual."

"Right away, sir."

As the day wore on, a peculiar pattern emerged. Various men arrived, each claiming a connection with Riot through an app, stirring the mansion into a frenzy of gossip and speculation. Confused, family members converged on Riot's room, each with their own blend of concern and curiosity.

His father was first. "Son, how are you?"

"What is it, dad?"

"Hold up, why you snapping, little nigga? I was coming in here to see—."

"I know why you here. So just keep it real."

"Okay, is there something you want to tell me?" He asked gently, ready to accept Riot regardless of the revelations that might follow.

"I'm straight, dad. This is a fucking game that I'm not a part of."

"Okay, son, just know that I'm here."

Riot fell backwards in bed and slammed a pillow over his face. But his peace was short lived with the arrival of his aunt, Minnesota, asking a bunch of questions too.

Riot didn't know when and he didn't know how but he had plans to get back at Patrick. And stop the games once and for all.

CHAPTER TWENTY

"She's taken things to a dangerous level."

Mason stood before the expansive window of his apartment, gazing out with a serious air, while River was perched on the edge of the sofa, her attention fixed on him. "You going to Walid's opening night at the club?"

"Nah, not in the mood." He shook his head. "I don't think anybody will be there. Definitely not Banks since he wanted us out the way."

"I'm sure Banks gonna have people all over that club."

"Facts."

River looked down and back at him. "Blakeslee looks bad. And I don't know what your plans are but...but you got to do something."

"She's not eating," Mason said taking a sip of his coffee. "That's her way to get back at me."

"Is it working?"

Silence.

"You know I'm gonna do whatever you want, but we have to weigh the pros and the cons."

"I know," he replied.

Turning to lean against the window, he thought about the situation. "I'm caught in a web of my own making," he admitted. "Despite what Banks might say, the thought of anything happening to her is unbearable otherwise I would have killed her a long time ago. I don't know if I'm getting soft or—"

"Nah, you on the right track." She moved closer. "This your friend's daughter. We gotta be smart. I mean, do you care about her?" She asked, probing deeper into Mason's feelings.

"I do, but..." Mason paused, lost in thought. "There was a moment she reminded me so much of Blair...or Blakeslee that I had this vision of what Banks might have been, had he not embraced his true self. And I know in my heart that she was the spitting image. So I let myself go."

River listened intently as Mason confessed.

"And when I had her, I realized she wasn't what I wanted. But by then, it was too late."

River shifted, a serious tone coloring her voice. "There's something you need to know. She's taken things to a dangerous level."

Mason's concern deepened. "What you mean?"

"I caught her attempting suicide. Well, she had the knife to her wrist and I grabbed it. But I'm not sure if I can catch her every time."

Mason sat his coffee cup down and paced, his mind racing. "What the fuck am I going to do with that girl? I can't keep her locked away, especially now that she's pregnant. And if Banks finds out the full extent of what's happening, it could be the end of us both."

"One way or another this is about to unravel. And I'm worried for you."

Mason exhaled. "Worrying about 'what ifs' won't change reality. I need to face this head-on." He inhaled and exhaled. "Keep an eye on her a little longer. I'll go to Banks and do what she's asked."

"What you mean?"

"Tell him the truth and deal with the consequences."

"Mason, I don't like that answer. I rather kill her ass and be—."

"I gotta step up, River. So I want you to watch her." He walked to the door, and something told him to look back. And when he did, he saw a look in her eyes he'd seen before.

Bloody murder.

"River, she's off limits. I don't want you to hurt her."

Silence.

"River, don't hurt her. I can see that look and this time I want you to stand down."

With all the love in her heart she said, "Are you sure?"

"I am." He exited and went to deal with his fate.

CHAPTER TWENTY-ONE

"To the man who deserves everything."

As Walid was chauffeured in his luxury Mercedes, he thought about his situation. He had successfully ruined the Falcon brothers so easily, he was somewhat disappointed that they weren't worthy adversaries. They didn't give up much fight and it was almost like they were as clueless on who was responsible.

If they did target his club, where was the fight back?

Especially after he dismantled their entire operation.

Glancing through the rear window, he spotted two cars shadowing him, a testament to his father's habitual overprotectiveness. He didn't feel like fighting it if he wanted to. Besides, he wasn't going anywhere but his club. So if they wanted to follow him inside, they could have at it.

With everything to celebrate, for some reason he didn't feel like he won.

Why not?

His club was opening, soft opening of course to get out the kinks. And his employees were happy and on top of the world. So why wasn't he pleased?

He knew what he needed and so he dialed Aliyah, just to hear her voice.

"Hello?" Her voice broke through, her tone light and unsuspecting.

"How you doing?" He asked, trying to hide the complexity of his emotions.

"I'm doing good. You sound..."

"What?"

"Well," she said sparking a glimmer of hope within him.

"Listen, baby, I'm gonna see somebody. About the shit going on in my head. And I don't...I don't know what it'll solve but I...I gotta find out what's going on with me and...I guess it's just fucking with my mind. And I—."

"It's okay, baby," she said. "Just you thinking about it, is enough for me." She hesitated a moment before saying, "Oh...I left something for you in the car."

Confused, he prodded further until Thomas, his driver, presented him with a watch box.

"When did you do this?"

"Last night. I found out from Banks and Mason that you were having a soft opening. So I...I just wanted to put a smile on your face."

Excited and surprised, he opened the box. Nestled within red velvet and adorned with a golden bow, lay an exquisite Rolex, its inscription reading, *"To the man who deserves everything."*

It was quite a thoughtful gift. And so he took off his current diamond stunner and slid it on. It fit perfectly. "This means a lot to me," he confessed, touched by her gesture, despite their strained relationship. "I'm sorry, Aliyah. Like, for real. You didn't deserve half of the shit I did to you and...and I just want you to know that I want you to be happy."

"You mean that?"

"I do. Even if it's not with me." His club came into view. "I gotta go. But I'll see you later tonight. Let's talk more."

The call ended as he arrived at his club, greeted by a throng of admirers and the elite of the DMV area. Amidst the celebration, his heart ached not just for Aliyah but for the realization of Ace's fate. He wasn't willing to let it burn that night, but he would finally deal with losing his brother, no matter how painful.

CHAPTER TWENTY-TWO

"They intend to demonstrate their seriousness."

In the shadows of the woods, Banks paced with a restless energy. The area illuminated by the headlights of an Escalade, signaled a meeting steeped in secrecy. As two additional cars glided into the clearing, Munro, and Joanne emerged from vehicles.

Swatting a few mosquitos Banks said, "What you find out? Was I right?"

Munro, his gaze shifting between Banks and Joanne, confirmed the suspicions that had been gnawing at Banks' soul. "You were right."

"The family of Celeste is behind the extortion and threats," Joanne added.

This realization meant once again, even in death, Ace was causing him problems.

Ace, the more tumultuous of the twins, had once lashed out in violence as a child and shoved Celeste down the stairs, leaving her paralyzed. A deed that haunted the family's legacy.

Banks had agreed to make amends, offering financial support for Celeste's healthcare, but his abrupt departure from the United States left those promises unfulfilled. And although he had gotten busy with his life, like Zoa said months earlier those left in the memories never forgot.

"How is Celeste?" Banks inquired.

"She passed away," Joanne disclosed, delivering the worst news.

"We believe that's what sparked this situation."

Banks, grappling with the information, felt a surge of irritation. The idea of being extorted over a tragedy that he tried to rectify was infuriating. Sure he understood their plight, but his family was off limits.

Period.

"There's more," Munro added, hinting at deeper layers to the drama.

Banks, already on edge, braced himself for further revelations.

"While researching this case, we got found out," he said.

"How?"

"They had been following us," Joanne replied. "But, Banks, unless this family is more powerful than you, something else is up. I think what's happening is a situation I've seen before."

"How so?"

"We believe Celeste's family went to a professional to get back at you for not giving them money for her healthcare. But when this professional realized the Wales was involved, they saw a bigger payday, and pretty much took over the case, giving Celeste's family the muscle they needed to press you harder."

"They also made it clear that our failure to uphold the initial agreement...the promise you made to Giorgio, had not gone unnoticed," Munro explained. "So they intend to demonstrate their seriousness."

"What does that mean?" He asked through clenched teeth.

"He did not say," Joanne admitted. "But we have every reason to be alarmed. Their message was clear and should not be underestimated."

Banks grabbed his cell phone from his pocket. He had to call his family and he had to call them now.

Danger was around the corner.

CHAPTER TWENTY-THREE

"My family tends to gravitate towards people like you."

The club was buzzing, a testament to Walid's vision coming to life on its opening night. The air was electric, charged by the grace of dancers who weaved through the crowd, their personalities as captivating as their movements.

Walid was in full boss mode doing all he could to make sure his clientele enjoyed their night and tipped heavy to make his employees happy.

He was in the zone, while unknowingly to him, a beauty stepped through the doors. It was Aliyah, a vision in white. Her thick black hair dripped down her back and her dress was adorned with diamonds that caught the light with every step. Her arrival was like a scene from a movie, drawing every eye in her direction.

Graciously accepting a glass of champagne from Whitney, the club's esteemed hostess, Aliyah was on a mission to find Walid. As she moved through the packed crowd, her demeanor was poised and serene. Her intention wasn't merely to attend. It was to reconnect with Walid, to weave back together the threads of a relationship frayed by misunderstandings and missed opportunities.

Outside of the mansion's walls.

A few minutes in, as fate would have it, their eyes met across the crowded room. Walid, drawn to her as if by a magnetic force, met her in the middle of the dance floor, his hand finding its place on the small of her back.

She was stunning.

How could he fumble her in the first or second place?

Oh yeah, she broke it off after he begged her not to leave.

And once his heart was destroyed, he sat a stone in its place.

"What you doing here?" Walid's voice was tinged with surprise. "I thought you were going to bed."

"I hoped you'd want me here," she said softly. "Tried calling you but—."

"My phone is on the charger."

She nodded and smiled when she looked down and saw the watch. "It fits perfectly." She grinned.

"I don't know what made you come tonight, but—."

She kissed him, their lips meeting for the first time in years. Separating from him she said, “Walid, I don't want this for us. I don't want us to argue or fight. I want us to raise Baltimore and Roman in the best circumstances possible.”

“What you really saying, Aliyah? I want you to be clear.”

“I want us to try again,” she said softly. “That is...if you aren’t—.”

“Still single,” he paused. “But I don't wanna talk about this right now. I want to be focused so I can give all of my attention to you. Where it’s quiet. And just us.”

“You want me to leave?”

“Looking like this?” He observed the beautiful dress. “Nah, we gonna enjoy the night.” He noticed the arrival of caterers carrying black insulated food bags. “But let me go outside to make sure everything is going smoothly with the food. We been waiting all night on this shit.”

“Of course.” She said kissing him again.

Once outside, as he approached the white truck to check on the additional deliveries, his attention was momentarily diverted by the logistics of the evening's catering. "How many more bags you got?" He longed to get back to Aliyah, so he wanted an answer quick.

A large, tatted man said, "Everything here."

"The lobster too?"

"Like I said...everything."

"Y'all charged me for the first event that didn't go down. I don't have a problem with it, but I want tonight to—."

BOOM!

A catastrophic explosion ripped through the night; the club was consumed by flames. The blast threw Walid against the truck with such force that it left an imprint of his body on the frame.

Dazed but determined, Walid tried to approach the inferno, and was rewarded with second degree burns on his arm. Banks' men grabbed him and held on tight but it didn't stop his fight. Over and over he attempted to enter until all of Banks' men tossed him in the car and drove away. One piloting the vehicle while the other prevented him from pouring out into the streets.

Walid was devastated.

Not from the loss of his dream but from the realization that Aliyah was gone.

Joey strolled down the bustling street, the woman he'd met online a few weeks earlier, Christy, was at his side. She wore a ponytail that bounced whenever she moved that he thought was cute. He was contemplating taking their relationship to the next level even wondering if she would be the one he'd introduce to his family.

As they walked towards his car, his arm casually draped around her shoulders, he said, "Be honest with me, why you single?"

Her white skin reddened due to blushing. "Why do men always ask that?" She grinned. "Like why do y'all feel like we need a man?"

"Fair enough," he responded.

"For real though, I haven't been looking, honestly. When I joined the app, I thought I'd find someone to hang out with for a few days, nothing serious. And then I met you." She confessed.

"By nothing serious, do you mean sexually?" Joey probed.

"You can say that," she replied, a note of honesty in her voice. "Is that a problem?"

“It’s different.” He hoped she wasn’t a whore. “I just appreciate your honesty,” he confessed as the city's traffic hummed around them.

“You sure you don’t think it’s weird?”

“Nah, like I'm thinking about introducing you to my family,” he said, his words carrying the weight of his intentions.

“You don't have—.”

“I know, but I want to.”

“Who is your family? Because you’re always so secretive about them.”

“You’ll find out soon,” he paused. “I will say this...you're straightforward, no games. My family tends to gravitate towards people like you.”

Her curiosity piqued, “So, when is this meeting going to happen?”

“We have a situation now but after—.”

His sentence was abruptly cut short as he was shoved into oncoming traffic by Christy. A tractor-trailer loomed ahead, its massive form bearing down on him with relentless speed. Before he could get out the way, the impact was immediate and he was struck on his left side, his body flying up in the air like a rag doll, before spinning to the right.

People screamed.

Some offered aid.

But the one person who should have helped was gone.

Christy.

Patrick had discreetly slipped away from the protective confines of his home, ignoring the warnings from his grandfather and the rest of the family about the dangers lurking. The way he saw it was simple. He was gonna go to his favorite food spot, grab something to eat and hit it back home.

Their safety measures were in effect, but Patrick's craving for the comfort of his favorite carryout...the one that honored him with a dish named the Patterson Wales...drew him onto the street like a roach.

Returning to his car, with his prized meal, Patrick was startled by an unexpected visitor. Marvel, who he last knew to be behind bars, slid into the passenger seat with an ease that annoyed him.

"How you doing?" She asked, as if their last encounter hadn't ended with police.

"I'm fine," Patrick replied, his voice low.

"What you get to eat?" She snatched the bag from him.

"Food."

"Drive, nigga," she commanded, looking through the bag.

As they drove, Marvel, between mouthfuls of rice, said, "So you didn't even bother to check on me, huh?"

"What you want me to do? You got arrested for check fraud. I ain't have nothing to do with that."

"You really don't give a fuck."

"That's not true," he protested. "I just got busy. You know shit crazy in my house. I ain't even supposed to be out now."

"You don't give a fuck about rules. Remember? I know you."

"What do you want?" He asked, annoyed.

"I wanna know why you didn't bail me out?" She challenged.

Caught off guard by the confrontation, Patrick confessed, "I did see about your bail. They said—"

"Stop lying!" Marvel's frustration boiled over, her voice raising. "You left me in that piss hole for hours!"

"I'ma be real with you," Patrick started, attempting to clarify himself. "I wasn't feeling how you were pushing up. Like, you started to believe we were really married and shit. And it wasn't fun no more."

"Nigga, I made you! You were a bum with a few coins before I fixed you up!" Marvel's response was sharp, her disappointment in his betrayal clear. "Now I'ma tell everybody in your family how you really feel."

Those were fighting words. "Don't do that!"

"Too late. All you had to do was see about me. So you brought this on yourself."

The conversation escalated until Patrick, driven to a desperate act at a stoplight, reached into his glove compartment and grabbed a knife.

Her eyes widened. "What you...what you about to—."

He stabbed her once, twice and many times in the chest. Before long the entire car was covered in blood splatter and puddles. As an onlooker from a neighboring car witnessed the scene, Patrick panicked, speeding away with Marvel slumped in the passenger's seat.

Dodging a truck in the process.

The remnants of blood clung to Patrick's frame as he approached Butter's apartment door. The pulsating neon sign from the corner carryout across the street, shined on him. Highlighting his murderous shame. He got most of the blood off his hands with a water bottle, but he needed more help.

He knocked several times, until Butter finally opened the door. His silhouette framed by the soft glow of his sparkling-like apartment. He was a vision in his satin red robe that caught the light with every move along with his extra glossy lips.

"Patrick, baby, what in the world?" Butter's voice was filled with concern. "Get in here."

The apartment, though tiny, was draped in fabrics smooth as liquid, walls adorned with vibrant art that spoke to Butter's flamboyant and gay soul. Patrick trudged inside and sank into a plush, velvet chair as Butter sashayed to the kitchenette, the clinking of a fine China tea set already steaming and ready to go.

"What happened?" Butter asked.

"I—I don't know, man. Marvel's got it twisted, thinking she's my wife and—."

"Y'all were still playing that game?"

"She wouldn't let it go," he said. "Why didn't she let it go?"

Butter, moving with a grace of a ballerina, brought over two steaming cups of tea, setting them on the table with a clink. “Drink this, honey. It's chamomile and it soothes the nerves.”

He eased next to Patrick, and he took a hesitant sip. “I'm worried. Shit went too far.”

Butter, his nails glinting, patted Patrick's hand. “Look at me, Patrick. You're gonna get through this. You always do. But why you here? I told you I’m not gonna play the game no more.”

“You still mad because—.”

“Yes! I’m still mad…you used me for sex and jokes. And then threw me away. But I won’t be—.” Butter frowned while looking at his shirt. “Hold up, is that blood?”

“Yes, but—.”

He grabbed the teacup and sat it down. “Ah, nah, honey you got to go.” He yanked him up with the strength of fifty niggas. The femineity thrown out the window.

“But I was—.”

“Now! All I need is police at my door. You gotta take care of this shit on your own.” He shoved him out and slammed the door in his face.

Riot had just said goodbye to his mother and Susie Q who, despite not being his girlfriend, he shared a connection. Their time together, along with moments spent with his twin brothers and mother, provided him with a sense of normalcy and safety. He was even considering moving in with Lila but didn't know how to break it to his father.

As he made his way to his car parked on the dimly lit street, a distance from his mother's front door, Riot's steps were halted by a voice. Turning around, he found himself face to face with a man dressed in jeans, a white t-shirt, and a black suit jacket.

"Did you say my name?" He asked suspiciously.

"Yeah. How you doing?" The stranger inquired, his demeanor oddly calm.

"What you want, nigga?" Riot asked, not in the mood for any games.

"I'm a friend of your mother."

"Okay, well, go inside. Why you out here talking to me?"

The stranger approached but kept his distance. "You don't have to be that way. I was just being nice.

I mean, did I do something to disrespect you?" He paused. "I'm Dedrick," he extended a hand.

Riot hesitantly shook it when without warning, Dedrick pulled Riot closer and tried to stab him. But Riot was quick, and thanks to the self-defense techniques he'd learned from his stepbrothers, he hit him with a blow to the nose, causing him to drink his own blood. Next, he punched him in the belly button, knocking the wind out of his soul. He was whipping his ass so much his man bun had unraveled and was very much giving the movie Grudge.

Eventually the knife spun on the ground and Riot took it away before raising his foot and bringing it down on the man's face, knocking him out cold.

Jumping into his car, Riot left Dedrick bloodied on the ground.

Mason's sleek Mercedes glided to a stop in front of the sprawling mansion, its headlights cutting through the night. He tossed the keys to the valet with a nonchalance born of habit not disrespect.

Tonight was a night of reckoning.

He even avoided Banks' calls because he wanted what was to be done, to be done in person. Face to face if you will. It would be a night where secrets would spill like red wine on white linen. As he unveiled a truth so heavy, it threatened to crush him and Banks in the process.

As Mason rounded the corner, the air buzzed with tense voices, whispers sharp as shattered glass. They were coming from the lounge.

Something else was wrong.

Concerned, he quickened his pace, and burst into the room. Banks, alongside two of his armed guards, turned at his entrance. The atmosphere was charged.

"Why didn't you answer your phone!" Banks yelled. "I was worried about you!"

"Sorry, I was hung up." He paused. "But what's going on?"

Banks closed the distance between them. "We're under attack. Joey's been hit by a tractor-trailer and fighting for his life in ICU."

Mason's heart skipped a beat. "What? How did...how did that happen?" He blurted.

But the blows kept coming.

"That ain't it. You have to sit down for this one."

"Nah, I'ma remain standing."

Banks sighed. "Walid's nightclub exploded with a bomb," Banks continued, his voice a low rumble. "He's alive, but Aliyah...she's gone."

"Hold up, Walid's okay right?" He asked repeatedly. He cared about the girl, but he needed to make sure that the only remaining son he had with Banks was still alive. "I did hear you say my son is okay right?"

"Yes, he's fine."

Mason felt the world tilt, his friend's words a gut punch that left him reeling. As he struggled to process the package of tragedies, his phone rang, slicing through the thick air. "Hello?" He answered, the word barely a whisper.

"Hey, it's River."

"Now's not a good time," Mason managed.

"It's about Blakeslee," River pressed on. "Remember I said she seemed off? It's worse. She lost her baby."

In a flash, Mason was moving, driven by a force he couldn't name. "Where you going?" Banks demanded. "Because I'm about to go to the hospital for—."

"Blakeslee had a miscarriage," Mason said, his voice strained.

Banks's brow furrowed. “A miscarriage! Why she calling you instead of me?”

Spacey entered just in time. “She tried, pops, but couldn't reach you. We ready to see about Joey?”

The room felt smaller, the air thicker as Banks absorbed the weight of the moment. “Uh, yeah, let's go.” Suddenly Banks' eyes hardened. “But just so y'all know, it's no more Mr. Nice Guy,” he declared. “From this moment, this family follows my lead! And that goes for everybody!”

Mason's heart pounded against his chest as he darted out of the mansion, the urgency of reaching Blakeslee propelling him forward. The night air, thick with tension, seemed to wrap around him, whispering of the turmoil he caused.

Once in front of the house, the sight that greeted him froze the very blood in his veins. His grandson Patrick was hunched in the driver's seat of his car. Beside him, Marvel's dead body was stiff and drenched in blood.

Was this shit real?

Mason approached the car, his steps slow, measured, as if navigating through a minefield. “What's going on?” He said his eyes rolling from the body back onto his grandson.

“G-pops, I need help,” his voice was a desperate plea.

Mason’s eyes widened and his hands pressed against the sides of his face. Was his bloodline that fucking dumb?

Yes!

“Did you drive on the highway with a dead body?”

“Nobody seen me.”

“You driving a three hundred-thousand-dollar car! Everybody seen yo ass! What the fuck happened?” Mason pressed. “Because from where I’m standing, it looks like a body in the passenger seat for no reason.”

“It was an accident. I...I snapped.” A heavy shroud of regret.

Confusion and dread tangled within him, a storm threatening to burst. There was no way he could leave him like that and yet he couldn’t stay. So he pulled his phone from his pocket and made a call to dispose of the body.

“We’ll be there in twenty. Tell him don’t touch anything else.”

"Get the fuck out," he said when he ended the call and arrangements were made.

When he was outside, he slammed his body into the car. Muscles and all, Patrick wasn't prepared for that grown man strength. "Listen, little ass nigga, I want you to stay the fuck in this house. First I want you to shower and put everything you got on in a bag and put it in the basement. Do you understand?"

"Yes, G-pops."

"If I find out you left, for any reason, I will break your jaw. I'm not fucking around," Mason added, his voice a cold, hard edge.

With a heavy heart, Mason retreated to his car, the engine's roar ripped into the quiet night. As he sped away, the mansion loomed in the rearview mirror.

Under the harsh fluorescent lights of the hospital corridor, Mason's steps were heavy as he approached her room. Once he arrived, he paused at the door and gathered his composure before entering the dimly lit space where Blakeslee lay, wrapped in white hospital linens. The moment their eyes met, she began to cry silently.

"I'm sorry, Blakeslee."

He moved closer, reaching out to touch her hand, but she snatched it away.

"I know you don't want to hear this, but I'm here for you," Mason whispered, his voice fragile and filled with guilt.

A few moments later, the door swung open, and Banks entered, his presence filling the room with an unspoken authority. He found it strange that his friend was there but approached his daughter's side anyway. "You okay?" Banks asked.

She looked at Mason. "Please leave. I want to talk to my father alone."

Retreating, Mason found himself back in the corridor, the weight of his hand in all of this pressing down hard. He was a man caught up in secrets and lies.

But he wasn't alone. Eight of Banks' men were also there. Ready and on guard.

After fifteen minutes, Banks finally emerged. "Come on. They letting us see Joey now. He's on another floor."

Why wasn't he angry?

Why didn't he say more?

Surely Blakeslee told him everything.

As they walked, the hospital's halls, for Mason it felt like they were walking the last steps of their friendship.

Forever.

The air in Joey's hospital room was thick with grief, a tangible cloak of despair that wrapped around each family member as they entered. The sterile beep of the heart monitor punctuated the silence, a relentless reminder that someone had tried to take out Joey.

Joey fucking Wales!

A staple in the family.

And now there he was. Motionless in the bed, eyes closed. Face bruised.

Walid, still reeling from the loss of his son's mother in the explosion, stood by his older brother's side. Before long Spacey entered. Unable to see his brother in that condition, he stood with his back in his direction, tears rolling down his cheeks. A rare moment of vulnerability for the man who was often the pillar of strength and jokes for his siblings.

Minnesota entered next and stood on the opposite end of Walid. She grabbed Joey's other hand for support. She had been crying so much that her makeup had streaked down, causing weird patterns on her face.

Banks and Mason entered last. Their arrival was serious. Not only were they positive that losing another son was not something Banks was prepared to do, but also the hallway was covered with more men than what was legally allowed. But Banks didn't give a fuck. The men were to remain on duty at all times because his safety would be a major priority.

Walking up to Walid, he gripped him from the back of his head and planted a kiss on his forehead. For a second, he held him so tightly, it caused him discomfort. But the idea of losing him in any way, was just as bad as Joey being in the hospital bed. He was legit relieved.

Mason came behind Walid, and gripped him so tightly Walid almost broke down, but held it together to remain strong.

Now was the hardest part.

Walking to the foot of the bed, Banks looked at Joey.

Bandaged up.

Broken.

Unconscious.

If he died monsters would take over Maryland. Of that everyone was sure.

The room seemed to shrink to accommodate the weight of their collective grief, each person in a shared pain that had come to define the Wales family.

For a moment, they simply existed together. Words were unnecessary. Their presence, the unity, spoke volumes.

Finally, Banks broke the silence, his voice cutting through the heavy air with authority. "I'm calling a family meeting in two hours," he declared. "Everyone will be there, or else."

Without another word, he stormed out, his departure as abrupt as his arrival. The room seemed to exhale in his absence, the tension momentarily eased.

With Joey being injured, the close call for Walid and Aliyah being dead, the Wales and Louisville families were at a crossroads.

Something had to change.

And that change would be brought on by Banks Wales.

CHAPTER TWENTY-FOUR

"I'm capable of deep dark things!"

In the shadowed grandeur of the mansion's boardroom, Banks sat at the head of the table. The heavy air of the fire in Belize still clung to him, a reminder of the warnings he had issued upon their return to the states.

"I told you all," he said. "This country doesn't want us here."

His cautions had gone unheeded, drowned out by the desires of each member now seated before him to flex in the US. Mason was at Banks' right, while Spacey, calm but uneasy, settled to his left. The room was filled out by Minnesota, Walid, Patrick, Bolt, and Riot.

"What we're facing," he declared, his voice a controlled thunder, "was orchestrated from a single source. And although I'm aware of the reason of this attack, I don't know the muscle that's driving it. That means we're still in danger. And you know how I deal with danger when it comes to my family." His eyes danced across their faces, each one averted, avoiding his scrutiny like it was a physical blow.

Spacey sat deeper into his seat.

Turning the conversation he said, "Other things have come to my attention," Banks continued. "So, tell me, what secrets are we keeping from each other? While I put out this larger fire, is there anything else that will be dragged to our doorstep?"

Patrick inhaled deeply. "I…I killed someone."

Everyone but Mason was shocked, having cleaned up the matter.

"Come again?" Banks said.

"I took care of it," Mason said. "They already removed the body, car and evidence early this morning."

Bolt was shocked that Patrick could go so far. And yet Riot had no problem believing he was capable.

"Why didn't you tell me?" Banks asked Mason.

"It happened as we were going to the hospital."

Suddenly Riot laughed out of pain and disgust at Patrick. "So, you a liar and a killer too?"

Patrick leaned forward. "What did you just say?" The threat in his voice heavy.

Riot shot back, "You've been faking around town like you a Wales. Thinking you'll get respect by using our name. But nothing you do gonna work. You forever gonna be trash."

Mason leaned in, his disappointment too much to bear, "Is this true, Grandson? Have you denounced our fucking name?"

Patrick, eyes moved downward. "I... I only did it for a while."

"He dropped out of college too," Riot continued. "And—."

"Why you snitching, son?" Spacey asked.

"Snitching? This nigga been fucking with me since day one. Sending gay men to the house. Trying to act like I like men. He even sent somebody to my mother's house to fight me."

"Hold up," Patrick frowned. "That wasn't me."

Riot sat back. For some reason he believed him.

"That was probably an attack connected to this war," Mason said. "But I'll deal with you later, Patrick."

He didn't know it now, but his credit cards and cars would be snatched by morning.

Patrick looked at Riot and said, "And I'll deal with you later."

After just beating the breaks off a nigga, Riot shot back, "When you feeling froggy I'll be ready."

"NO!" Banks brought a hand down on the table. "We're not going at each other." He looked at Mason. "Not at this time!"

Everyone settled.

Banks, ever the general, moved the interrogation on, "Who else?" His eyes settled on Walid.

"Father, you know what I have going on."

Banks nodded, a gesture of understanding amid the chaos. "We need to be transparent here."

Minnesota leaned forward and placed her clasped hands on the table. "I've been building a place... for me and Sugar. I can't do this drama anymore."

Banks was incensed. "Are you leaving us when we're at war?"

"We always at war," Minnesota pled. "And nothing matters to me more than Sugar, so I have to see to it that she's safe."

"You can do what you want," he lied, "But if you do, my granddaughter stays here. She has Wales blood in her veins so that makes her a soldier. Ain't shit she can't handle."

The room, already charged with tension, felt the added strain of Banks' ultimatum.

"That's not fair," Minnesota trembled.

"And yet it don't change a mothafuckin' thing!" He rose. "No one here should be shocked that I would act this way. I never wanted to return to the States. And this is what I got for relenting. I won't do it again. You will follow my lead or every nigga in here will die! And trust me, I'm capable of deep dark things!" He walked to the door and paused. "Oh yeah, I've already ordered a first round of attacks."

As Banks stormed out, the air was thick with threats and promises.

CHAPTER TWENTY-FIVE

"You aligned yourself with the wrong people."

In the bustling heart of the city, an unexpected spectacle unfolded. A vibrant balloon truck, adorned with colors as vivid as a painter's palette, made its way down the street.

The destination?

Celeste's people.

The Glass family members who made an ill-advised attempt to target the Wales clan was in deep trouble. And now, as a result a delivery was in route. Each trip was planned to the letter.

The first stop was Marcus Glass' barbershop, where the buzz of clippers and talk about nothing filled the air. That is until a white man in all red walked into the doorway holding a bouquet of balloons. "I have a delivery for Marcus!" He said with a smile. His voice broke the monotony.

The shop fell silent as Marcus, walked up to the man. "For me?"

"Yes, sir. Enjoy."

The man walked out as quickly as he entered. A minute later, as Marcus read the card, the balloon popped, releasing a cascade of fire in his face. Since the explosion was controlled, killing only its recipient, with the exception of a few bumps and bruises everyone else was okay.

The patrons erupted into screams as they witnessed Marcus lying dead on the floor.

Next stop was Brandon Glass.

In the midst of laying down a new track in the studio, he had to pause when a balloon delivery momentarily stole the spotlight from his music.

"Delivery for Brandon Glass," the man announced.

"It ain't my birthday," he said taking the delivery anyway.

Just as quickly as the messenger came, he left. And just like before, it concluded with an explosion, ending the life of Brandon Glass.

Banks was relentless and far from done.

His hit list was not all over the place. Every member of the Glass lineage participated in the downfall of his family and so he would react in larger form.

Next was Felicia Glass, who Banks learned, along with her mother, was in charge. And so, in the sleek and sanitized halls of her tech company, a balloon delivery was on the way.

"Bring it in," she said excitedly, believing it was her mother celebrating the recent hit on the Wales family.

And so, when the balloon basket was placed on her desk, everyone was in horror when the explosion caused the same fate.

Her life.

Jordan and Tyler Glass also fell victim and if Banks had more names he would hit them too. He was not playing games and continued until he was satisfied that they knew who they had fucked with.

As for Jasmine and Maya Glass, after learning about the fates of their family, their day took a darker turn, when they were forced into the opulence of a Maybach. The vehicle, a symbol of Banks Wales' influence, was a departure from the mundane life they were accustomed. This made it all the more ridiculous considering they chose to go after a family with so much power. They should have been smarter. In their minds he was a businessman not a killer.

They were wrong.

And so, in the car they held onto each other.

They weren't stupid.

They knew who came calling. What they didn't know was what would happen to them at the end of the destination in such a luxurious ride.

In the cold expanse of an abandoned warehouse, Jasmine Glass and her daughter Maya stood shivering. Within moments Banks, Mason, Spacey, and Walid entered their presence applying pressure on their mood.

Wearing smoke grey slacks and a soft black T-shirt, Banks approached. "I'm sure you understand why we've gathered you here," his voice bounced off the walls.

Jasmine trembled. "Yes, but you have to understand, you left my daughter alone! Abandoned her! When you promised to take care of her bills. She died because of your son!"

Banks nodded. "My personal affairs overshadowed my attention to your daughter, true. But had you sought me out, the shit that went down with your family would not have. This is your fault!"

Mason stepped forward. "You aligned yourself with the wrong people. Now you know better."

Jasmine took a deep breath. “At this point, you stripped everything from me. There's nothing left to fear.”

Walid interjected, “Because of you, I ruined the life of two men who had nothing to do with the closing of my club. And then you went harder and had it blown up!”

“I wanted to—.”

“They killed my son’s mother!” He roared, causing Mason to place a hand on his son’s pounding heart.

Jasmine stood stoically, the air around her crackling with hostility.

“What other chaos did you plan?” Banks pressed. “Come clean and your only living daughter may survive.”

Jasmine looked down. “Everything that has happened to you over the past few weeks, months, was probably us.”

Banks knew it but had more questions for Jasmine. “You've lost everyone but Maya. Are you prepared to lose her as well?”

Jasmine shook her head and looked at her only remaining child. “I’m not. What do you need from me?”

Banks issued a chilling warning. “Your compliance is noted, but any deception from here on out will have painful, torturous consequences far beyond your darkest nightmares."

"You have shown me what you can do. So tell me what I can do for you to leave us alone."

In the aftermath of the tense meeting, Banks led Mason, Spacey, and Walid towards a location that seemed to exist in whispers and rumors alone. Sunset Haven was its name, and it was a place that promised security and luxury far removed from everyday life.

This is the house that Banks built.

As they approached, the entrance to Sunset Haven revealed itself to be deceptively simple, a hidden door that blended seamlessly with its surroundings. It looked like a luxurious home, not unlike any place they lived in before.

But once inside, the quartet descended into the depths of an underground cavern that was more epic than the world above. Designed to withstand any calamity, Sunset Haven was a testament to Banks's foresight and determination to protect his people at all fucking cost.

As they walked deeper, the underground dwelling unfurled like a subterranean palace, with fourteen rooms each bearing the stamp of luxurious living. The air was fresh, recycled through systems that mimicked the natural environment outside.

"This is our next step," Banks declared, his voice echoing off the walls of the underground marvel. "Above ground will be a part of our everyday lives. But until we find out who funded the Glass family we will retreat here at night."

The men looked at one another in disappointment and awe. Knowing that even if they went to another island, whoever was behind the Glass attack, would probably find them there.

"Let me show you more."

They wandered through the pool hall, its tables untouched but ready for use. Next, they encountered the pool, its waters still and inviting under the artificial glow. It was an oasis of calm, and for some reason they were relaxed.

Next, he showed them the lounge and then the library with shelves laden with books that offered escape and enlightenment.

"Sunset Haven isn't just about survival," Banks continued. "Here, we're untouchable. Here we plan, we strategize, and we protect what's ours from those who seek to destroy us before we destroy them first."

After Sunset, Walid sat slumped in the dim light of the car's interior. He couldn't bother to drive and so he sat in the back, looking out of the tinted window. Everything was a blur of color, as his thoughts crashed against one another. After all, last night his son's mother was murdered in his club, leaving him in a sea of grief.

Suddenly his phone erupted with a vibration in his pocket. Reluctantly, he reached for it, expecting another wave of condolences or tragedies.

But this message was different.

It was a text from Minnesota who had tried calling to no avail when he was in the tunnel.

Brother they pulled out Aliyah! She's alive!

Time stopped.

The words on the screen seared into his consciousness. Disbelief and relief waged war in his heart and he felt reborn.

"Take me to the hospital! Now!"

"Right away, sir!"

Upon arriving at the hospital, Walid's steps echoed through the sterile halls, each one a beat closer to Aliyah. The door to her room stood before him and as he entered the sight of her lying there, so still yet so alive, stole his breath away.

It wasn't Aliyah who they found dead in the explosion.

It was Cynthia, who managed his club and resembled her closely.

Slowly he approached her bedside, hoping it wasn't a lie. If it was, he couldn't take it, that was for sure.

But there she was, breathing with the help of machines but very much alive. Even the faint burns and bruises didn't take away from her beauty. Her leg was in a cast and her arm too, but again, she was alive.

"Aliyah," he whispered. "I thought...I thought I lost you, baby."

The moment stretched into eternity, as he hung onto every breath she took. And then, a miracle. Her eyelids fluttered and her gaze met his.

"Baby," he began, his voice cracking with emotion, "You don't know what I been through. I...I can't believe you're alive."

She smiled.

But her eyes fell closed once more.

As Banks navigated through his mansion, he mentally ticked off the whereabouts of his family members. With Walid, Minnesota, Spacey, Blakeslee, Joey, and Mason all being accounted for at the hospital, a sense of relief washed over him, knowing that the remainder of his circle was safely within the walls of his home.

However, upon entering the living room, Banks was greeted by an unexpected sight that brought a sudden halt to his stride.

There stood Zoa.

He would be lying if he didn't say it, but seeing her face brought him relief.

"Hey there, stranger," she said, her voice soft and sweet.

Banks found himself momentarily lost for words, overwhelmed by the emotions her presence stirred within him. "Wow, this... this really got to me," he managed to say.

"A good thing I hope."

"It is."

Zoa approached, closing the distance between them with a few graceful steps. She reached out, taking his hands into her own. "When I found out about what was happening to your family...to people I consider family too...I had to cut my trip short."

"Why didn't you tell me?" Banks asked. "I would've sent for you."

"Spacey and Mason made the arrangements. We didn't want to bother you."

"I can't believe they did this." He held her in his arms. "But you know the saying in this house? Everybody loves Zoa," he laughed softly.

The laughter faded as Zoa's expression softened, her eyes meeting his with an intensity that spoke volumes. “I'm so sorry, honey. I'm so sorry that you had to deal with this alone.”

“I'm not really alone. I have family,” Banks responded. “But...you know how that is too. For now, I have to play the villain.”

“Let's catch up,” she suggested. “Update me on what's happening, how you're feeling, but more importantly, what you need from me. Because if you'll have me, I'm not going anywhere.”

CHAPTER TWENTY-SIX

"Let's let her decide who she wants..."

In the sterile tranquility of the hospital room, Walid reentered, his steps muted against the polished floor. A breeze fluttered through the open window, casting Aliyah's face in a serene light. He had been out speaking with the Falcon brothers in the cafeteria, to make things right after first believing they were responsible for fucking with his club. They were surprised he even reached out, and after offering enough money for them to get back on their feet and more, they were made whole.

That was the most solid shit they'd ever seen in their lives.

He was about to sit at her side when the sudden sound of a toilet flushing snapped the room back into reality. Walid glared in confusion as he turned toward the source of the noise. From the bathroom emerged a figure, his skin a deep shade of Hershey chocolate, a contrast to Walid's own.

"Who are you?" Walid demanded.

The stranger offered a brief chuckle. "You must be Mr. Wales," he said, amusement in his voice.

"I asked you a question, and I expect an answer."

"My name is Josh. Josh Fisher. You can consider me Aliyah's man."

Was this nigga crazy?

He made his way toward the bed with a confidence that irked Walid's soul.

Josh's claim of being Aliyah's boyfriend may have drawn a brief laugh from Walid, but it still stung. Besides, Walid knew the depth of his connection with Aliyah, their tangled history, and how his own actions allowed another man to snake through.

As Josh settled beside Aliyah's bed, Walid moved closer to him. Through clenched teeth he said, "Let me tell you how this is going down. You're going to get up, get the fuck out, and never contact her again. Understand?"

"And if I don't?" He challenged, the air between them charged with more aggression.

Walid, brushing Aliyah's face with the softest touch, made his position clear, "I'm not in the habit of not getting what I want. So if you contact her again, you'll be sucking your own dick. And then I'll chop off your head."

Josh rose and straightened his suit jacket. He paused, as if to touch Aliyah, only to be stopped by

Walid's stark warning, "You touch her and you die right here. Right now." As if they could feel his temperature, two Wales security men entered the room.

Josh acknowledged them and looked at Walid. "You say you love her right?"

Silence.

"Well if that's true, isn't she smart enough to make her own decisions? I mean look at the life you have her in. This feels dangerous. Doesn't she deserve better?"

"My patience is wearing."

"Let's let her decide who she wants when she wakes up. Shall we?" Josh replied, before making his exit, leaving Walid simmering with rage.

CHAPTER TWENTY-SEVEN

"He's no one. Just like me."

Mason stepped into Blakeslee's hospital room, his heart heavy with guilt. The room, bathed in the soft glow of the evening, cast shadows that seemed to accentuate the dark circles under her eyes. Once vibrant and full of life, her skin now bore a look of grey.

Upon hearing Mason's approach, she turned her head. Once their gaze met, she quickly averted her eyes. "What do you want?"

"I'm going to admit everything to Banks," Mason declared.

Blakeslee giggled. "You know, I'm quite aware that this is mostly my fault," she said. "I not only played a role in us being together, but I pushed for it so hard, despite one simple fact."

"What's that?"

"My pussy was wet enough, but you didn't care about my heart."

"Blakeslee, it's not like—"

"Please, don't interrupt me," she begged. "I need to say this. I'll tell you your part in this horror in a moment."

He shook his head.

"Despite everything, I clung to the hope that you might change your mind. Yes, you saw me as nothing more than a plaything, but at the time, that was enough for me. It showed how desperate I was for any form of connection with you, or any human really. Now, what I'm left with is..."

"What?"

Her voice faltered as she delivered the most crushing news. "I can no longer have children. So now, I'm worth even less."

Mason listened, each word a dagger to his heart.

"And you, your actions isolated me further. Without even the cold stares or whispers from my family and then you, I'm truly invisible."

As they spoke, a nurse entered the room, her appearance marking a transition. "Are you ready, Ms. Wales?" She asked gently.

"I am," Blakeslee confirmed as the woman helped her out of bed.

"Where is she going?" Mason inquired, a note of panic in his voice.

“To a mental facility,” the nurse answered, her tone clinical and to the point.

“A mental facility? For what?”

“I’m sorry, but who are you again?” The nurse turned to him, seeking clarification.

“He's no one. Just like me,” Blakeslee interjected, her words cutting through Mason like a knife.

As she was wheeled out of the room, Mason was left standing alone. The realization that Blakeslee's life was ruined and that he was a part of it, didn’t sit right with his soul. And he doubted it ever would.

CHAPTER TWENTY-EIGHT

"I'm willing to let this slide right now if you are."

Patrick and Bolt were chilling in the backyard, fully aware that rolling out without Banks' say-so was now completely off the table. Banks made it crystal clear, with threats and bodily injury.

No one was to leave the mansion without his approval.

And no one did.

Hell, Patrick had no money. No car. For him there was nowhere else to go.

So, Patrick and Bolt were kicking back, enjoying the good life in luxury. The chef was firing up some barbecue and the air was thick with the scent of grilling, and the sound of the latest music from male and female rappers. They didn't have a care in the world as the music thumped through the speakers.

Life was smooth, until Riot showed up.

Patrick, who'd been beefing with Riot non-stop, shot him a look as Riot stared him down for blood. "Fuck wrong with you?" He asked as Riot stepped closer.

"You said you would deal with me later," Riot declared, straight up, no chaser. "So here I am."

Patrick was thrown, not expecting this kind of call-out. "Get out my face before I hurt you."

"You've been on me about nothing for years. So here I am, right now, no longer scared of you. Fuck do you wanna do?" He cracked his knuckles.

Patrick, never one to back down, shrugged it off and stood up. "Remember this shit is on you, not me."

Boxing was Patrick's game since way back, so for him, it was whatever. But the moment Patrick moved, Riot was on him, landing a quick blow to his right jaw. Patrick, feeling the sting of embarrassment, tried to come back, but Riot was slick, dodging and weaving, before hitting Patrick in the eye.

Now Patrick was afraid.

Because no matter what he tried, he was coming up short. Riot successfully kept him off balance and Bolt was no help. After seeing how he dropped Dallas weeks ago, he already knew the man was different so unlike Patrick, Bolt left him alone.

Blow after blow Riot was the more dominate and serious about standing his ground. Causing Patrick to feel weak and stupid.

Pushed to the edge, and in severe pain, Patrick charged, full tilt. But he wasn't ready for what was next. As he ran toward Riot like a charged bull, he shoved him backwards.

But there was a barbell left out in the open and Patrick tripped over it and crashed down hard to the ground. To make matters worse, right before his fall there was a loud snap, stemming from his leg. He had broken his femur.

As the commotion drew a crowd, Riot stepped up to him, reached behind himself and pulled out the curly wig and lipstick. He sat it on his head and smeared the makeup all over his face.

The staff was stunned as the man continued to scream in pain while Riot chose violence. Far from sorry he said, "Shhh...shh. This on you not me. I'm willing to let this slide right now if you are. But if not, I'll be ready and waiting."

"Bolt, go tell my aunt you found her wig!"

"Okay!" He yelled and ran into the house.

With that, Riot dipped back into the mansion, leaving Patrick and the staff to the business as they tended to his leg and ego.

Riot was deep in conversation on FaceTime with Suzie Q, who was trying on a variety of outfits with an excitement that was contagious. She had gotten an interview as a customer service rep, hopefully ending her tenure on Only Fans and she was excited.

"Nah, don't go for that one," Riot instructed, his eye for style kicking in. "Grab the peach blouse and those white pants."

"This one?" Suzie Q held up the outfit, seeking his approval.

"Yeah, that's the one," Riot confirmed.

She quickly changed into the selected outfit and did a little twirl, her arms raised in the air. "What you think?"

"You've been hired, "Riot declared, a hint of pride in his voice.

Suzie Q couldn't contain her glee, breaking into a dance. "Riot, you really have changed my life. Like even if I don't get this job, I will always be grateful to you."

"What you mean?" He asked, genuinely curious.

"Before you, I didn't really care how I looked. On the site they wanted me with my clothes off anyway. But now people do a double take when they see me. I feel like I'm seen," she explained.

"I may have helped you pick out clothes, but you've always been beautiful," Riot reassured her, his sincerity clear. "And smart. Don't let nobody take that from you."

"I know, but it really is different now. People look at me with more respect. I just wish...you were..."

"What?"

"I wish you were into me," Suzie Q confessed.

Riot paused. Though he hadn't seen her in that light before, he found his perspective shifting a bit. At the same time it didn't mean he would change his stance. "I can't make any promises, Suzie. And I don't want to lead you on. We aren't blood, but there's the family dynamic to think about. One that I take very seriously," he explained cautiously.

"Yeah, our parents would flip if we got together in real life," Suzie Q acknowledged. "But I'm willing to take that chance if you are."

"If it didn't work, and I lost you it would hurt. So...so let's just enjoy the moments we have together for now. Will that work for you?"

"Okay but promise me one thing."

"I'm listening"

"That you'll seriously consider fashion design. I know you're in college for computer tech because of your grandfather's wishes."

"Yeah, everyone's following his path except Patrick, who chose medicine."

"A doctor?" She yelled. "I wouldn't let him come near me with a 10-foot pole." Suzie Q laughed harder. "But seriously, how would your granddad react to you switching majors?"

"It's tough to say," Riot mused. "But it's my life. I need to live it for me."

"So, when can I see you again? I've discovered this new Mediterranean spot we've got to try."

He thought about Banks. "Not sure. But as soon as we're clear, you'll be the first person I want to see."

CHAPTER TWENTY-NINE

"You mentioned a pound of flesh."

As Sharon Drexel looked at the trees out the large window, she now understood what they wanted and who they were.

Over 48 hours, she was treated to five-star meals, fresh water, and regular bathroom breaks by her captors, a treatment far removed from the stark brutality often associated with abductions.

Initially, Sharon's spirit was cloaked in despair, the victim narrative playing in her mind. However, as the hours passed and stories unfolded, a realization dawned upon her.

She was to blame.

"So, you know who I am?" She ventured, her voice cutting through the tension-filled room where four men stood, their gazes locked on her. "And the fake bid was—"

"Just a way for us to find out about every friend, family member and even the consultation clients who ever hired you."

"Smart." She took a deep breath. "May I turn around Mr. Wales?"

Suddenly two men grabbed her by the arms, turned the chair and pushed her back down. There in the room was Banks, Spacey, Walid and Mason.

"You know who I am but let me make this official. I'm Banks Wales, and you've been aiding the Glasses in tormenting my family."

"Please, don't take it personally," Sharon attempted to deflect. "When they came asking around for help to get revenge, I made myself known to her. It had always been business."

"Having quite a few companies myself, I understand the notion of business. But you fucked with my family. So for me, all this shit is personal."

Mason stepped up. "You could've been on the opposite end of this shit, told us what was up and gotten more money. But you chose otherwise."

"And because of you and your men, my son Joey lies awake yet immobile in a bed. Robbed of his ability to walk or even turn his head."

Walid dragged a hand down his face. "You were also behind the explosion at my club, leaving my son's mother with scars that mar her face for life."

Sharon shook her head, her attempt to maintain innocence crumbling. "I'm well aware of what I did. But do you think you're any less culpable, with all your money and power?" She looked at all of them. "You have hurt many, for less reasons!"

Banks acknowledged her point, "I've hurt many, but never for less. And that doesn't make this any easier for you. I don't give a fuck what I do out there, you don't touch me or mine."

The conversation spiraled.

"And it's time to face the repercussions," Banks declared. "But it's not too late. You will give us everything we need and more."

"What do you want from me?" Sharon yelled, the weight of her situation bearing down on her.

"You're brilliant. The way you were able to help the Glass family while also laying back and out of the way was perfection. Finding men with no social presence also something I haven't seen before. But what I really want is the list."

"What list?" She whispered.

"The one that includes everyone who has a vendetta against us. I became aware of this list very recently, since returning to the states."

"You see, we know niggas too," Mason smiled.

"I want to stop these people before they come at us. No longer am I willing to be on defense."

"We attacking first," Walid added.

Banks laid out his demand, revealing more details of their interest in Sharon. Her unique ability to unearth those determined to remain hidden along with the list gave her value. But they also told her about her family and friends and everything she had done in the past week, all without knowing she was being followed and filmed. Her life could be touched.

When they were done, she was spent emotionally and very afraid. "And what if I don't give you this list? What then?"

Banks' response was cold, calculated. "Then everybody you fucking love, including your mother, will die."

Faced with an ultimatum, Sharon resigned. "Please don't. I'll tell you everything you want to know." And then she remembered something. "You mentioned a pound of flesh."

"Yes," Banks said.

"What did you mean?"

"You attacked my family, people got hurt. And so I decided I want to be the only man in your life. So that nigga you been keeping time with is gone."

With tears rolling down her cheeks, in the shadowed corners of the room, using the pen and ink, she wrote down every name she could remember.

While understanding that her life would never be the same.

EPILOGUE

Sunset Haven buzzed with an air of complex emotions swirling inside. Banks, Mason, Patrick, Riot, Bolt, Walid, Blakeslee, Sugar, Minnesota, Spacey, and Joey, who was in a hospital bed, settled into a comfort and danger. Aliyah was awake but still recovering in the hospital.

Comfortable, if something popped off, they would be good.

But dangerous because the haven allowed for a situation that if Banks desired, he could lock each of them inside and no one would know. Or have access. At the end of the day his yearning to keep them safe also made them feel unsafe.

They were all sitting in the living room trying to pretend that all was cool. Blakeslee, on the other hand, had yet to speak to Mason and to keep the peace he avoided her as well.

Suddenly, Banks, amid the muted conversations and clinking glasses, surveyed his family. "I'm happy we're all here," he began. "It's been tough, but like Spacey said, honesty and vulnerability will make us the strong unit I know we can be. The Louisville's and the Wales', together as one." The room erupted in cheers.

Mason, glass raised, caught Banks' eye.

"Now, if you don't mind, I'd like some time alone with my old friend."

"Sure, dad," Minnesota replied, her voice soft with affection.

"Whatever you want, pops," Spacey echoed.

As the room emptied, leaving Banks and Mason in the quiet comfort of their sanctuary, Banks moved to the bar with an ease born of countless similar evenings. "Who's thirsty?" He joked, an expensive whiskey in hand.

Mason's response was light, "I am," as he prepared their cigars, a ritual that prefaced their moments in the past.

Seated in their recliners, positioned as always directly across from one another, they settled into the familiarity of their friendship. This setting, whether in Belize, the States, or underground was always the same.

"Everything appears to be going great," Mason observed, breaking the comfortable silence.

"You and I both know that nothing is ever as it seems."

Mason nodded. "True. But it feels like the family understands why we must be here, at least until we find our enemies."

"I agree," Banks concurred. "Until we deal with those on the list, we have to alternate our time from here and above."

"Agreed," Mason nodded.

And then, with a slight shift in tone, posed a question that he wanted and answer to immediately. "But speaking of enemies, can you tell me this...Is it true that you're fucking my daughter, nigga?"

The glass fell from Mason's hand, shattering the peace.

The Cartel Publications Order Form

www.thecartelpublications.com

Inmates **ONLY** receive novels for $13.00 per book **PLUS** shipping fee **PER BOOK.**

(Mail Order **MUST** come from inmate directly to receive discount)

Shyt List 1	________	$15.00
Shyt List 2	________	$15.00
Shyt List 3	________	$15.00
Shyt List 4	________	$15.00
Shyt List 5	________	$15.00
Shyt List 6	________	$15.00
Pitbulls In A Skirt	________	$15.00
Pitbulls In A Skirt 2	________	$15.00
Pitbulls In A Skirt 3	________	$15.00
Pitbulls In A Skirt 4	________	$15.00
Pitbulls In A Skirt 5	________	$15.00
Victoria's Secret	________	$15.00
Poison 1	________	$15.00
Poison 2	________	$15.00
Hell Razor Honeys	________	$15.00
Hell Razor Honeys 2	________	$15.00
A Hustler's Son	________	$15.00
A Hustler's Son 2	________	$15.00
Black and Ugly	________	$15.00
Black and Ugly As Ever	________	$15.00
Ms Wayne & The Queens of DC **(LGBTQ+)**	________	$15.00
Black And The Ugliest	________	$15.00
Year Of The Crackmom	________	$15.00
Deadheads	________	$15.00
The Face That Launched A Thousand Bullets	________	$15.00
The Unusual Suspects	________	$15.00
Paid In Blood	________	$15.00
Raunchy	________	$15.00
Raunchy 2	________	$15.00
Raunchy 3	________	$15.00
Mad Maxxx (4th Book Raunchy Series)	________	$15.00
Quita's Dayscare Center	________	$15.00
Quita's Dayscare Center 2	________	$15.00
Pretty Kings	________	$15.00
Pretty Kings 2	________	$15.00
Pretty Kings 3	________	$15.00

Pretty Kings 4	__________	$15.00
Silence Of The Nine	__________	$15.00
Silence Of The Nine 2	__________	$15.00
Silence Of The Nine 3	__________	$15.00
Prison Throne	__________	$15.00
Drunk & Hot Girls	__________	$15.00
Hersband Material **(LGBTQ+)**	__________	$15.00
The End: How To Write A Bestselling Novel In 30 Days (Non-Fiction Guide)	__________	$15.00
Upscale Kittens	__________	$15.00
Wake & Bake Boys	__________	$15.00
Young & Dumb	__________	$15.00
Young & Dumb 2: Vyce's Getback	__________	$15.00
Tranny 911 **(LGBTQ+)**	__________	$15.00
Tranny 911: Dixie's Rise **(LGBTQ+)**	__________	$15.00
First Comes Love, Then Comes Murder	__________	$15.00
Luxury Tax	__________	$15.00
The Lying King	__________	$15.00
Crazy Kind Of Love	__________	$15.00
Goon	__________	$15.00
And They Call Me God	__________	$15.00
The Ungrateful Bastards	__________	$15.00
Lipstick Dom **(LGBTQ+)**	__________	$15.00
A School of Dolls **(LGBTQ+))**	__________	$15.00
Hoetic Justice	__________	$15.00
KALI: Raunchy Relived (5th Book in Raunchy Series)	__________	$15.00
Skeezers	__________	$15.00
Skeezers 2	__________	$15.00
You Kissed Me, Now I Own You	__________	$15.00
Nefarious	__________	$15.00
Redbone 3: The Rise of The Fold	__________	$15.00
The Fold (4th Redbone Book)	__________	$15.00
Clown Niggas	__________	$15.00
The One You Shouldn't Trust	__________	$15.00
The WHORE The Wind Blew My Way	__________	$15.00
She Brings The Worst Kind	__________	$15.00
The House That Crack Built	__________	$15.00
The House That Crack Built 2	__________	15.00
The House That Crack Built 3	__________	$15.00
The House That Crack Built 4	__________	$15.00
Level Up **(LGBTQ+)**	__________	$15.00
Villains: It's Savage Season	__________	$15.00
Gay For My Bae **(LGBTQ+)**	__________	$15.00
War	__________	$15.00
War 2: All Hell Breaks Loose	__________	$15.00
War 3: The Land Of The Lou's	__________	$15.00
War 4: Skull Island	__________	$15.00
War 5: Karma	__________	$15.00
War 6: Envy	__________	$15.00
War 7: Pink Cotton	__________	$15.00
Madjesty vs. Jayden (Novella)	__________	$8.99
You Left Me No Choice	__________	$15.00
Truce – A War Saga (War 8)	__________	$15.00
Ask The Streets For Mercy	__________	$15.00

Truce 2 (War 9)	$15.00
An Ace and Walid Very, Very Bad Christmas (War 10)	$15.00
Truce 3 – The Sins of The Fathers (War 11)	$15.00
Truce 4: The Finale (War 12)	$15.00
Treason	$20.00
Treason 2	$20.00
Hersband Material 2 **(LGBTQ+)**	$15.00
The Gods Of Everything Else (War 13)	$15.00
The Gods Of Everything Else 2 (War 14)	$15.00
Treason 3	$15.99
An Ugly Girl's Diary	$15.99
The Gods Of Everything Else 3 (War 15)	$15.99
An Ugly Girl's Diary 2	$19.99
King Dom **(LGBTQ+)**	$19.99
The Gods Of Everything Else 4 (War 16)	$19.99
Raunchy: The Monsters Who Raised Harmony	$19.99
An Ugly Girl's Diary 3	$19.99
From Men To Monsters (War 17)	$19.99

(**Redbone 1** & **2** are **NOT** Cartel Publications novels and if **ordered** the cost is **FULL** price of $16.00 **each plus shipping**. **No Exceptions**.)

Please add **$7.00** for shipping and handling fees for up to **(2) BOOKS PER ORDER**. (INMATES INCLUDED) (See next page for details)

The Cartel Publications * P.O. BOX 486 OWINGS MILLS MD 21117

Name: ______________________________

Address: ______________________________

City/State: ______________________________

Contact/Email: ______________________________

Please allow 10-15 BUSINESS days Before shipping.

****PLEASE NOTE DUE TO COVID-19 SOME ORDERS MAY TAKE UP TO 3 WEEKS OR LONGER BEFORE THEY SHIP****

The Cartel Publications is NOT responsible for Prison Orders rejected!

NO RETURNS and NO REFUNDS
NO PERSONAL CHECKS ACCEPTED
STAMPS NO LONGER ACCEPTED

Made in United States
North Haven, CT
01 April 2024